Clown Killer

Shane Reed

Copyright

Chapter 1

Marlene Thompson lounged on the flower-patterned sofa, legs tucked beneath her. The living room was bathed in the soft glow of the evening sun, filtering through half-drawn curtains. Across from her, Daniel leaned forward in his armchair, his hands clasped, eyes bright.

"Caught a break in the Henderson case today," Daniel said, a spark of excitement in his voice. "Looks like we might actually wrap this one up sooner than expected."

"Really? That's wonderful news!" Marlene's smile radiated pride. She watched her son, taking in his animated expression as he recounted the day's events.

Their conversation meandered to plans for the evening—a quiet dinner at home, maybe a movie later. Simple joys. Marlene relished these moments, a respite from the chaos that often surrounded them.

"Daniel," she began, her tone softening, "you know how much I love you, right?"

He nodded, a half-smile on his face, waiting for her to continue.

"Your father and I—we're so proud of who you've become. You're caring, determined." She paused, her eyes searching his. "And after everything that's happened, your strength amazes me every day."

"Mom, come on," Daniel replied, but his cheeks tinged with a hint of red, touched by her words.

"Never forget it, okay?" Marlene's voice held an urgency, as if trying to imprint her feelings upon his heart. "No matter what life throws at us, we're a team. You're not alone."

Daniel reached across the space between them, giving her hand a reassuring squeeze. "I won't forget. How could I with you as my mom?"

They shared a smile, a silent exchange of mutual affection and understanding. In the safety of their living room, amid the humdrum of suburbia, mother and son found their sanctuary.

Marlene fiddled with the gold band on her finger, a silent harbinger of worry etching lines across her forehead. "Daniel," she said, the words catching slightly in her throat, "your dad's been working late so much these days. It worries me."

Daniel turned towards her, his gaze sharp and focused. He noted the way her hands wouldn't stay still and how the laughter had faded from her eyes. "I know, Mom. I see it too."

"Sometimes I think he's married to that dealership more than to me," Marlene half-joked, but the smile failed to reach her eyes. Her vulnerability was palpable in the room, a thick cloud that threatened their momentary peace.

Daniel leaned forward, his voice steady and sure. "I'll talk to him," he promised. "He needs to remember what's important. Family. You. Me."

"Can you?" Hope flickered in Marlene's eyes, mixed with the weariness of countless nights spent alone.

"I can, and I will." His jaw set with resolve. "Dad listens to me, at least when it comes to business. Maybe it's time he listens about family too."

"Thank you." Relief washed over Marlene's features, softening the hard lines of concern. "You've always been my rock, Daniel."

"Always," he affirmed, the word a silent vow hanging between them.

Marlene's laughter floated through the living room, a balm to the earlier tension. She clutched her stomach, eyes brimming with mirth. "Do you remember when your father tried to fix the sprinkler system?" she gasped between chuckles.

Daniel couldn't help but join in, the memory vivid and absurd. "He was drenched before he even found the leak," he said, recalling the sight of his father, soaked from head to toe, swearing at the rebellious water spouts.

"Water geysered like it was Old Faithful." Marlene wiped a tear from her eye, her smile lines deepening. "Your dad stood there, baffled, while the lawn turned into a swamp."

"Never seen him admit defeat so fast." Daniel shook his head, his own laughter subsiding as he pictured the soggy aftermath. It was one of those rare moments when their family's imperfections had woven them closer together, sealed by shared hilarity.

The sound of a knock cut through the quiet aftermath of their laughter. Marlene and Daniel exchanged puzzled glances, the remnants of their smiles fading into uncertainty. Who could it be at this hour? The clock on the mantle ticked ominously, marking the seconds as they both stared at the door.

Marlene rose, her footsteps cautious as she approached the door. The warmth of family laughter still lingered like a fading echo behind her, but now each step seemed to be met with the creaking of wooden floorboards, speaking of her unease. She paused, hand hovering over the doorknob, her heart knocking a steady beat against her ribs. Curiosity pricked at her, mingled with an undercurrent of confusion. Why would anyone come calling unannounced?

"Probably just a neighbor," she whispered, more to quell the rising concern than out of any real conviction. Her fingers wrapped around the cold metal, taking a deep breath before turning it. A draft of evening air brushed her face as the door swung open.

There, on her porch, stood a figure so out of place it took a moment for her mind to process the sight. A clown, in full garish regalia, towered before her. Oversized shoes planted firmly on her welcome mat. A white-painted face stretched into a grotesque smile, eyes hidden beneath a tumble of red curls. His costume—a patchwork of too-bright colors—jostled absurdly as he held out a bunch of balloons in one gloved hand and a bouquet of wilting flowers in the other.

Marlene's breath hitched; her pulse throbbed in her throat. Something primal within her screamed that this was wrong, the painted visage before her not a harbinger of joy but an omen. The silent suburbia around her felt suddenly oppressive, every shadow a potential threat. Her voice, when it came, was a tentative whisper, betraying none of the alarm that skittered through her veins.

"Can I help you?"

The clown's silence stretched, too long and thick. Marlene's heart pounded a frantic beat as her smile faltered. She peered closer, trying to glimpse the person behind the makeup. The scent of latex and face paint floated in the air, mingling with the faint odor of sweat. It was all wrong; clowns belonged at birthday parties, not on her doorstep after dusk.

"Is there something you need?" she pressed, her voice firmer now, but it trembled slightly with unease. There was no responding chuckle, no cheerful mime act that would dispel the tension. Just the stillness of a pantomime gone awry.

Her eyes darted to the balloons, to their garish reflection of the porch light. The hand that held them did not shake, did not show any sign of the joviality one might expect. And then it happened—so swiftly, so unexpectedly—that the world seemed to tilt on its axis.

The bouquet dropped to the ground, petals fluttering like the wings of distressed birds. In one fluid motion, the clown's other hand emerged from the voluminous folds of his costume. Metal glinted, a stark contrast to the absurdity of his attire—a gun, its barrel unerringly pointed at Marlene.

"No—" was all she could choke out, the word dissolving into the quiet evening air.

A flash, a deafening crack shattered the serenity of the suburban night. Pain exploded in her chest, bright and searing. Marlene's knees buckled beneath her as she grasped at the wound, blood warm between her fingers. Her brown hair, once framing her face with gentleness, now splayed across the floor in disarray. She looked up, eyes wide with shock, seeking an explanation in the clown's inscrutable gaze.

But there was none forthcoming. Only the painted smile that didn't reach those hidden eyes, eyes that watched her without mirth as she collapsed onto the hardwood floor of her own home. The balloons, released from the clown's grasp, rose toward the ceiling in a slow, eerie dance. They were the last things Marlene saw before darkness edged her vision, the world fading to black amidst the echo of her son's name in her mind.

Daniel's world spun, the laughter that had echoed moments ago now a grotesque mockery in his ears. "Mom!" he screamed, the word tearing from his throat as he lunged toward Marlene, crumpled and still. His hands, shaking with an adrenaline-fueled tremor, fumbled for his phone. The digits 9-1-1 were a lifeline, one he punched into the screen with frantic urgency.

"Please, send help," Daniel pleaded, voice cracking as he tried to compress the wound with quivering hands. "My mom's been shot." Address spilled out in a staccato rhythm, the operator's calm voice a distant hum against the roaring in his ears.

"Stay with me, Mom. Stay with me," he begged between sobs, though Marlene's eyes remained glassy, unseeing. Blood seeped through his fingers, warm and relentless. He pressed harder, desperate to stem the tide, to rewind time to when their biggest concern was dinner plans.

"Daniel, the ambulance is on its way," the operator assured him, but the words felt hollow, empty. He knew. Despite the pulsing hope that drove each compression, part of him recognized the irreversible truth—life slipping away beneath his touch.

A shadow loomed at the periphery of his vision. Daniel dared a glance up, heart lurching at the sight of the clown. No longer the harbinger of mirth, but of death. Standing still, the painted grin more sinister than ever.

"Who are you?" Daniel's voice was a ragged growl, but the clown didn't respond. Instead, with a tilt of the head, as if acknowledging some private joke, the figure turned and stepped out into the dusk.

"Stop!" Daniel's command was lost to the void, his body anchored to his mother's side by a force stronger than gravity—the bond of blood, of love unyielding. As the sirens wailed in the distance, Daniel's gaze followed the retreating silhouette until it blurred into the encroaching night.

The sound of approaching sirens futile against the silence that had settled over her. The clown, a specter of chaos, vanished into the suburban labyrinth. And in the quiet living room, a son's world shattered, leaving only the echo of a question unanswered, the promise of a hunt just beginning.

Chapter 2

Marlene Thompson lounged on her worn, beige sofa, the glow from the television casting flickering light across the living room. She clutched a mug of chamomile tea in one hand, its warmth seeping into her palms. The other held the remote loosely, thumb idly pressing the volume button down. A crime show droned in the background, actors playing out fictitious horrors that no longer seemed so distant to her.

Her eyes, however, were not fixed on the screen but on a photo frame perched on the mantelpiece. It depicted a family, her family, entwined in an embrace that spoke more of protection than of mere affection. Her gaze softened as she traced the outlines of their smiling faces, the glass cold and smooth under her fingertip.

The room was steeped in a silence that was not quite comfortable, but Marlene had grown accustomed to it, the weight of solitude less oppressive with each passing day. It had become her refuge, a bulwark against the chaos that lurked just beyond the safety of her four walls.

A loud knock shattered the stillness.

Her heart leapt. The mug in Marlene's grasp nearly slipped from her fingers, tea sloshing precariously close to the brim. Eyes wide, she snapped her head toward the door. Her pulse thrummed in her ears, a staccato rhythm that matched the sudden surge of adrenaline.

"Who could it be at this hour?" she murmured, the question barely audible over the thudding of her heartbeat.

The knock came again, more insistent this time. Marlene set the mug down with a quiet clink against the coffee table, her movements deliberate, an attempt to steady trembling hands. She rose to her feet, the familiar comfort of her home now tinged with an edge of trepidation.

Marlene's footsteps fell soft on the plush carpet, each one measured, a stark contrast to the urgent knocking that had prompted them. She paused, hand hovering over the door handle, her breath catching in the stillness of the hallway. The knock echoed again, a demanding rap against the wood that set her nerves jangling.

"Stay calm," she whispered to herself, a mantra to quell the unease that tightened her chest. Her fingers curled around the cold metal, a slight tremble betraying her composure.

She glanced through the peephole, her eyes straining for a glimpse of the visitor. A colorful swirl met her gaze, disjointed and puzzling. Marlene's brow creased in consternation; this was no ordinary caller.

Taking a steadying breath, she unlatched the chain with a faint click, the sound magnified in her heightened state of awareness. Her hand pushed the door open, the hinges creaking softly, a slow reveal that pricked at her senses.

There he stood. A clown, grotesquely out of place amidst her quiet suburban existence. Balloons bobbed in one hand, a garish bouquet clutched in the other, their bright hues mocking the dusk's creeping shadows.

Marlene's eyes widened. Her lips parted, a silent gasp dissipating into the quiet foyer. A clown? Here? The absurdity of the sight before her clashed with the serenity of her evening ritual. Confusion knit her eyebrows together as she scanned the figure from oversized shoes to the frizzy wig crowning its head.

"Can I help you?" The question emerged more as a reflex than genuine inquiry, her voice laced with incredulity. This had to be a mistake, some sort of mix-up or perhaps a misguided attempt at a joke.

But the clown did not speak. Instead, it tilted its head to one side, studying Marlene with an intensity that belied the jovial image it presented. The silence stretched taut between them.

The clown's mouth, a caricature of joy in bright red paint, stretched wider. The twisted grin unnerved her—there was no warmth in it, no mirth. It was a leer, contorted and chilling, promising nothing of the laughter clowns were meant to bring.

Marlene's pulse quickened. This was wrong. Dangerously so. Every instinct screamed at her to shut the door, to lock out this garish harbinger of malice.

"Who are you looking for?" she ventured again, her voice a notch higher, betraying her mounting alarm.

Still, the clown said nothing. Its grin seemed permanent, etched onto the white canvas of its face—a signal of intent that Marlene couldn't quite decipher but instinctively feared. The flowers and balloons, once whimsical, now felt like props in a play she didn't understand, one where the stakes were all too real.

A flash of silver. Marlene's eyes widen. The clown's hand moves, quick as a whip-crack. Metal glints—a gun.

"Wait—" Her plea cut off.

Bang!

The sound rips through the calm evening, an ugly intrusion. It bounces between the houses, shattering the safety of the suburban cocoon.

Marlene jerks back, a puppet yanked by an unseen string. Her mind races, disbelief colliding with reality.

No time to think. No time to understand.

Fear grips the neighborhood in an icy fist. Silence follows the blast, heavy and foreboding.

Blood blooms like a grotesque flower on Marlene's blouse, crimson spreading over the delicate fabric. Her breath catches—a sharp intake that never fully escapes. Disbelief paints her features more profoundly than any makeup ever could. She stares at the vibrant stain, her fingers trembling as they touch the wound, tentative and unsure. Pain radiates, sharp and unyielding, from the epicenter of her injury. It's a foreign sensation—too intense to fully grasp, too real to ignore.

"Daniel," she whispers, the name a lifeline she clings to amidst the surging tide of shock.

Her son, her boy, stands frozen. Time seems to warp around him, every second drawn out and laden with dread. His mother, the pillar of his existence, wavers before him, her strength ebbing away in a flow of red. Daniel's eyes mirror the horror etched across Marlene's face. A wordless scream builds in his throat, muted by the paralyzing grip of fear.

Marlene's knees buckle, her body no longer hers to command. She falls, a marionette with severed strings, her world tilting into chaos. The floor rushes up to meet her, and she braces for impact, but the pain is distant, muffled by the adrenaline flooding her veins.

"Mom!" Daniel's voice finally breaks free, raw and laced with terror. He lunges forward, his own safety an afterthought. His hands reach for her, desperate to undo what has been done, to rewind the last few seconds that have fractured their reality.

The clown, the harbinger of this nightmare, stands as if rooted to the doorstep—an observer to the tragedy unfolding. Its twisted smile remains unchanged, a silent mockery of their despair.

Daniel cradles Marlene, his mind racing even as his heart threatens to shatter. His gaze locks onto the clown, a silent vow forming in the depths of his soul. Justice, retribution, vengeance—they swirl within him, a storm waiting to be unleashed.

But for now, he holds his mother close, her life's warmth slipping away between his fingers.

Daniel's hand scrabbled for his phone, the sleek surface slipping against his sweat-slick palm. He fumbled, once, twice, the device clattering to the floor in a taunt of wasted seconds. His breath came in sharp bursts, each inhale a knife to his chest, every exhale a tremor that threatened to unmake him.

"Come on, come on," he muttered, snatching the phone up again. His thumb jabbed at the screen, digits blurring as he willed the call to connect.

"9-1-1, what's your emergency?" The voice, calm and dispassionate, was a lifeline thrown into churning waters.

"Shooting!" The word burst from Daniel, a bullet in its own right. "My mom—she's been shot. Please, send help!"

"Sir, I need you to stay calm and give me your location."

"42—Linden Street. Hurry!" His voice cracked, the edges fraying with panic.

"An ambulance is on the way. Can you apply pressure to the wound?"

Daniel's eyes darted to Marlene, her stillness a silent scream. "I—I'm trying. Please, just hurry." The urgency thrummed through him, a drumbeat pulsing in time with her weakening heartbeat.

"Keep her awake if you can. Talk to her."

"Mom, stay with me." The plea was a whisper, a prayer flung into the void. Daniel's hands were red, his soul painted in the same hue, the color of desperation staining everything it touched.

"Help is coming, Daniel. Stay with me on the line."

"Please be fast," he choked out, the words heavy with a son's love, a protector's failure. He clung to the phone like a lifeline, the thin thread that connected them to a flicker of hope in the encroaching darkness.

The clown's back faced them, a silent mockery in its retreat. Balloons bobbed with false cheer while Daniel's heart hammered against his chest—echoes of a terror too raw, too real. Marlene lay motionless, her labored breaths the only sign she clung to life.

"Mom!" Daniel's voice broke, a plea lost to the void. The phone slipped from his grasp, skittering across the hardwood floor. He knelt beside her, hands shaking, blood smearing his skin—a crimson betrayal.

"Stay with me," he whispered, but the words fell flat, swallowed by the thickening silence.

Outside, the neighborhood slept, unaware. No barking dogs, no car alarms—just the distant wail of sirens, a promise too distant to soothe.

He looked up, the clown's twisted grin etched in memory. It turned the corner, its departure as enigmatic as its arrival. A chill settled in Daniel's bones, the night air creeping through the open doorway.

"Help is coming," he murmured, more to himself than to Marlene. But the confidence he sought was a stranger, an unwelcome guest in the chaos.

Daniel's gaze lingered on her face, the warmth that once radiated now dimming. Her eyes fluttered, struggling against the pull of darkness. He could almost hear her heart, every beat a fading drum in the symphony of life.

"Please." It was a word spoken countless times, yet never with such weight.

Footsteps crunched on the gravel outside—a countdown to salvation or despair. Daniel clenched his jaw, the metallic tang of blood a bitter reminder of their reality.

"Mom, you have to hold on."

But as the room spun and lights flashed through the windows, Daniel knew. He knew that some promises were fragile things, shattered in the blink of an eye. He felt it in the stillness that began to settle, in the quiet that grew louder with each passing second.

Chapter 3

Detective Brian Hayes' piercing blue eyes flicked up from his desk as the door to his office swung open. Officer Jessica Lee stood there, her posture rigid with urgency, a sheaf of papers clutched in her hands. His gut tightened; that look meant trouble.

"Got a new one, Detective," Jessica said, her voice steady despite the undercurrent of energy. "Homicide case."

Brian nodded, pushing himself up from the worn leather chair that had molded to his form over countless late nights. He noted the slight tremor in her hand as she handed over the file. The weight of it felt familiar, yet every case brought its own brand of darkness. He was ready.

"Who's the vic?" Brian asked, thumbing the file open and scanning the contents with practiced speed.

"Marlene Thompson," Jessica replied, her ponytail swaying as she leaned in to study the photos over his shoulder. "Suburbia. Mother of two."

He absorbed the information: kind-hearted, cautious, mid-40s. Her life seemed unremarkable until tragedy painted it in stark, bloody strokes.

"Let's go see what we got," he grunted, already heading for the door. Jessica fell into step beside him, her notebook out and pen poised.

"Detective Hayes, one more thing," Jessica interjected, her tone holding a note of disbelief Brian rarely heard from her. "Witnesses last saw Marlene speaking to a six-foot clown."

Brian stopped dead in his tracks, turning to face her. For a moment, nothing stirred in the sterile hallway—just the buzz of fluorescent lights overhead. A clown? It seemed ludicrous. Absurd leads were part of the job, but this?

"Are you yanking my chain, Lee?"

Her brown eyes met his, earnest and dead serious. "I wish I was, Detective. Bright red wig, white face paint, the works."

Frustration knotted between his shoulders. Clowns—a child's entertainer turned into a caricature of horror by popular culture, and now a lead in Marlene Thompson's murder investigation. Brian clenched his jaw, feeling the challenge settle upon him like a heavy cloak.

"Alright," he exhaled sharply, regaining his composure. "Let's canvass the neighborhood. Someone must've seen something."

They moved through the station with a brisk, determined pace. Whispers and sidelong glances from other officers bounced off them like rain on pavement—they were a force unto themselves, their reputation for closing cases a shield against doubt.

"Six-foot clown," Brian muttered under his breath, shaking his head. Yet, as they stepped out into the crisp air of the city, his mind raced. No detail was too small, no lead too strange. They'd work with what they had, however improbable. They always did.

Brian shuffled the crime scene photos, his fingers flicking through them with practiced ease. Beside him, Jessica leaned in, her gaze sharp and probing. The stark images—a life violently ended, a room awash with chaos. And yet, somewhere within this morbid puzzle lay threads of truth.

"Back to square one," Brian grumbled, his blue eyes scanning each photo. "Every witness we've got is spooked by that damn clown getup."

"Maybe it's misdirection," Jessica suggested, her voice steady despite the absurdity. "Could be a ploy to draw attention away from something—or someone—else."

"Could be." Brian acknowledged the possibility with a nod. His mind worked methodically, sifting facts from fiction. He knew the devil lay in the details.

"Let's map out what we know," she said, pulling out a whiteboard. With a marker poised, she recapped the knowns: time of death, entry point, lack of forced entry.

"Means they might have known our vic," Brian interjected, "or had access."

"Or Marlene let them in." Jessica added a question mark next to 'access'. Her hand moved swiftly, jotting down other pertinent notes.

"Right." Brian's tone was clipped as he picked up another photo—a wider shot of the living room. Something about the placement of a lamp, knocked askew but not shattered, caught his eye. A detail, previously unseen.

"Look at this," he pointed. Jessica peered over. "Lamp's tilted, bulb's intact. Odd for a struggle."

"Controlled chaos?" Jessica pondered aloud, adding it to their growing list of queries on the board.

"Exactly." Brian's pulse quickened, a silent drumbeat urging them forward. He tapped the photo. "And no smudges on the paint. Our clown wore gloves or cleaned up."

"Which means premeditation." Jessica's ponytail swished as she nodded, her thoughts aligning with his. "They planned it, wanted no trace left behind."

"Except for the costume." Brian's voice carried a note of irony now. "Big risk, big statement."

"Which means it's personal?" Jessica ventured, her brown eyes reflecting the challenge ahead.

"Or meant to send a message." Brian's jaw set firmly. "Let's find out which."

Notebook in hand, Jessica stood on the Thompsons' porch, Brian beside her. They exchanged a glance before she rang the bell. It was answered by Marlene's sister, Clara, eyes rimmed red with grief.

"Detective Hayes, Officer Lee," Clara nodded, voice barely above a whisper. "Come in."

Inside, the air was thick with sorrow. Brian cut straight to the chase. "We need to know about Marlene's friends, anyone who might hold a grudge."

"Marlene?" Clara shook her head, bewildered. "She was loved by everyone. No enemies."

Jessica scribbled down notes, empathetic but focused. "Any unusual encounters? Someone dressed oddly?"

"Like a clown?" Clara's brow furrowed.

"Exactly." Brian pressed on.

"Nothing. I—It's absurd."

"Thank you, Clara." Jessica's words were soft but firm. "We'll do everything we can."

They moved from house to house, gathering fragments of Marlene's life, searching for inconsistencies. Friends recalled a warm woman, neighbors spoke of kindness, but no one mentioned clowns.

"Dead end after dead end," Jessica murmured, frustration mounting.

"Patience," Brian reminded her, eyes scanning the street. "The devil's in the details."

Their next stop was the crime scene. Yellow tape fluttered in the breeze as they ducked under it. The living room was still a tableau of the macabre event.

"Let's go over it again," Brian said, his gaze sweeping the room.

Jessica pulled on latex gloves, stepping carefully around the space. Each surface told a story, each item a potential clue. She studied the disarray, looking for anomalies.

"Nothing here is random," Brian mumbled, kneeling by the lamp.

"Agreed," Jessica responded, circling the space. Her eye caught on a bookshelf, titles askew. She approached, scanning the spines.

"Anything?" Brian asked, joining her.

"Maybe," she replied, her finger hovering over a gap between novels. "This looks intentional. A book missing, perhaps?"

"Good catch." Brian's approval was evident. "Could be part of a message."

"Or a trophy," Jessica added, her mind racing with possibilities.

"Let's canvass again," Brian decided. "Someone saw something."

"Back to square one," Jessica acknowledged, determination etched on her face.

"Sometimes," Brian said, stepping back into the daylight, "that's exactly where you find your breakthrough."

Brian Hayes tapped a rhythm on the steering wheel, his blue eyes fixed on the precinct ahead. Jessica Lee rifled through a stack of folders beside him, her ponytail swinging with each movement.

"Clowns," Brian muttered, more to himself than to his partner. "Never thought I'd be hunting one."

"First time for everything," Jessica replied without looking up.

They stepped into the squad room, the buzz of activity a stark contrast to the quiet they left behind at the crime scene. Brian headed straight for his desk, flipping open his laptop with practiced ease.

"Reaching out," he announced, fingers flying over the keys as he drafted emails to various agencies. "If anyone's seen this before, we'll find them."

"Got it," Jessica said, nodulating as she picked up the phone, dialing numbers from a list of experts in abnormal criminal behavior.

"Detective Hayes and Officer Lee," she introduced, voice steady, "working a homicide with an unusual aspect—a clown."

Brian watched her, noting the furrowed brow as she listened, absorbing information. He sent off another email, then glanced at the clock. Time was slipping away, and Marlene's killer was still a mystery wrapped in a colorful, nightmarish costume.

"Anything?" he asked once she hung up.

"Mostly theories. One suggested checking circus troupes, street performers." Jessica frowned. "But it feels off."

"Keep digging," Brian encouraged, knowing her tenacity would turn up something sooner or later.

They moved to the row of monitors set up in the corner of the room, where surveillance footage from the area around Marlene's house awaited. The grainy images flickered across the screens, showing the comings and goings of a suburban neighborhood unaware of the horror that had unfolded within it.

"Here." Jessica pointed to a timestamp hours before the estimated time of death. "Could be nothing."

"Or everything," Brian added, leaning closer. A figure passed by a house, too far to discern details, yet its gait seemed... deliberate.

"Zoom in on that," he instructed, his gut tightening.

Jessica worked the controls, enhancing the image as much as the resolution would allow. It was blurry, but the outline was unmistakable—a tall figure, an exaggerated silhouette.

"Looks like we've got our clown," Brian stated, the words heavy with implications. "Now let's find out where it came from."

"Tracking its path," Jessica affirmed, already queuing up additional footage, her earlier frustration now replaced with focused resolve.

"Good work," Brian said, watching the screen intently. "Let's unravel this."

The clown's appearance on camera was brief, but it was a lead—something tangible in a case that felt like grasping at smoke. Together, they watched the figure move through the shadows of the neighborhood, both knowing that every second they spent staring at the past brought them one step closer to catching a killer hidden behind a painted smile.

Brian Hayes's fingers flew across the keyboard, the clack of keys a staccato rhythm in the otherwise silent precinct office. Beside him, Jessica Lee leaned over a sprawl of documents, her brown eyes darting back and forth as she cross-referenced names and dates. They were digging into Marlene's inner circle, starting with her husband Mike.

"Mike's clean, at least on paper," Brian grunted, scanning the results of his background check. "No priors, stable job, alibi checks out."

"Friends and coworkers?" Jessica asked, flipping through interview transcripts.

"Nothing but shock and grief." He swiped through digital records on his screen. "And condolences."

Jessica's lips thinned into a line. "Someone's lying," she said. The determination in her voice matched the resolve in her posture.

"Clowns don't just materialize out of thin air," Brian muttered. He pushed back from the desk, his suit stretching over broad shoulders. "Let's hit the streets."

The afternoon sun cast long shadows as they stepped into the first costume shop, a bell jingling above the door announcing their arrival. Shelves lined with masks and wigs watched them as they approached the counter.

"Detectives," Brian announced, badge in hand. Jessica did the same, her movements sharp and practiced.

"Can we take a look at your sales records?" Jessica's request was more polite than necessary—a stark contrast to the gravity behind it.

"Sure thing, officers," the employee replied, nervously tucking a strand of hair behind an ear as she led them to the register.

"Anything... unusual sold recently?" Brian inquired, his blue eyes scrutinizing the employee's face for any telltale flicker of recognition.

"Unusual? It's all pretty standard—" she faltered under his gaze, "except, well, there was this one clown costume."

"Details," Brian demanded, his tone leaving no room for hesitation.

"Big order," she continued, tapping through the computer. "Paid cash. Picked up in person."

"Description," Jessica pressed, already anticipating the next step.

"Six-foot, maybe taller. Kept to himself. Wore a baseball cap, sunglasses. I remember because it struck me as odd."

"Odd how?" Brian prodded.

"Who wears sunglasses inside?"

"Got anything else on him?," Jessica asked, her pen poised over her notepad.

"Sorry, that's it. But he did seem... anxious."

"Thank and keep quiet about this," Brian instructed, handing her his card. "Call if you remember anything else."

"Will do, detective."

Outside, Brian and Jessica exchanged a glance. The clown costume was a lead, but it was thin—too thin.

"Back to square one?" Jessica's voice betrayed a hint of frustration.

"Not yet," Brian said, his jaw set. "We push harder. Someone knows something."

"Then let's find that someone," Jessica agreed, her determination reflecting in her stride as they moved on to the next shop.

Brian shuffled the crime scene photos across his cluttered desk, each image a macabre puzzle piece. Jessica leaned over his shoulder, her brown eyes scanning for overlooked clues.

"Clown shoes in the foyer," she muttered. "That's our point of entry."

"Or staged to seem that way," Brian countered, tapping a finger against the glossy surface of a photograph. He glanced at her, his blue eyes sharp and calculating. "What kind of killer dresses up to commit murder?"

Jessica pulled back, arms folded. "Psychological angle? Maybe the costume was a message."

"Or a smokescreen," Brian suggested, his voice low and steady.

"Marlene's past," Jessica said, a new thought dawning. "Could be tied to an old grudge."

"Except everyone loved her," Brian argued. "The community's still reeling."

"Everyone has secrets, Brian," Jessica reminded him, her tone firm. She picked up another photo, this one of Marlene's smiling face. "Even Marlene."

"Let's think outside the box," Brian proposed, standing up. "Could the clown angle be a red herring?"

"Possible," Jessica acknowledged. "But if it is, we're missing the real motive."

"Let's present what we've got," Brian decided. "We need fresh eyes on this."

They gathered their notes and made their way to the briefing room, where skepticism hung heavy in the air like stale cigarette smoke.

"Detective Hayes, Officer Lee," Captain Reynolds greeted them, not bothering to mask his impatience. "What have you got for us?"

Brian placed the evidence photos on the table, spreading them out. "Our perp wore a clown costume. Could be a ploy to throw us off."

"Or just a sick joke," someone from the back muttered.

Jessica stepped forward. "Background checks on the husband and close associates turned up clean."

"Too clean?" Reynolds raised an eyebrow.

"Nothing concrete yet," Brian admitted. "We checked costume shops, tracked down a sale matching our description."

"Great, so we're looking for a needle in a haystack," Reynolds scoffed.

"More like a clown shoe in a city of sneakers," Jessica said, undaunted.

"Pressure's mounting," Reynolds warned them. "Media's having a field day with the 'Killer Clown' angle."

"We're narrowing down the leads," Brian assured him, his jaw tightening. "This isn't going cold on our watch."

"Make sure it doesn't," Reynolds shot back. "Or it'll be your badges on the line."

"Understood," Brian responded, the urgency clear in his voice.

"Good," Reynolds said curtly. "Dismissed."

Outside, the two shared a look, the challenge set before them as glaring as the midday sun. The clown was their lead, and they'd follow it to hell if that's what it took.

Brian's fingers drummed a staccato rhythm on the steering wheel as they pulled away from the precinct. Beside him, Jessica stared at the passing cityscape, her brow creased in thought. Silence hung between them, heavy with unspoken frustration.

"Clowns," Brian muttered, breaking the silence. "Never thought I'd see the day."

Jessica turned to him, her eyes reflecting the streetlights. "We've seen worse leads." Her voice was firm, but he could hear the undercurrent of doubt.

"Marlene deserved better," he said. The image of her gentle smile, now forever lost, fueled his resolve.

"Her family..." Jessica's fingers tightened around the case file. "They're counting on us."

"Pressure is part of the job." Brian's gaze was steely as he navigated through traffic. He had faced down killers, negotiated with hostage-takers, but the invisible weight of expectation always bore down hardest.

"Every victim deserves justice," Jessica replied, echoing the creed that had been drilled into her since the academy.

"Right." Brian nodded. They were more than just officers of the law; they were the last line of defense for those who could no longer speak.

"New plan?" Jessica asked, ready to shake off the doubt and dive back into the fray.

"First light, we hit the streets again. Talk to every shop owner, every vagrant, anyone who might have seen something we missed." Brian's words sliced through their uncertainty.

"Expand the search for surveillance footage," she suggested. "Someone must've seen the clown outside of Marlene's neighborhood."

"Exactly." Brian felt the familiar thrill of the hunt rekindle within him. "We'll canvas the area, turn over every stone. Clown can't hide forever."

"Let's dig deeper on Marlene, too." Jessica rifled through her notes. "A detail, a connection, anything we overlooked."

"Every piece matters." He acknowledged her tenacity with a nod. Jessica's drive, often relentless, was what made her an invaluable partner.

"Tomorrow, we start fresh." She met his gaze, her determination mirrored in his own.

"Fresh," Brian agreed. The road ahead was uncertain, the case as bizarre as they come. But Detective Brian Hayes and Officer Jessica Lee wouldn't rest until the killer clown was unmasked and Marlene's memory honored with justice served.

"Justice for Marlene," Jessica whispered, almost like a prayer.

"Justice for Marlene," Brian echoed, his hands steady on the wheel as they drove into the night, their resolve unwavering despite the darkness that surrounded them.

Chapter 4

Detective Brian Hayes strode through the sterile corridors of the forensic lab, his piercing blue eyes scanning the environment with practiced ease. Officer Jessica Lee kept pace beside him, her ponytail swaying with each determined step. They rounded the corner, and Dr. Laura Evans came into view, her black hair a stark contrast to the white walls of the laboratory.

"Dr. Evans," Brian greeted, his voice cutting through the quiet hum of the lab equipment.

"Detective Hayes, Officer Lee," she replied, nodding at each in turn. Her blue eyes were steady, a mirror to Brian's own.

"Thanks for meeting us on short notice," Jessica said, her tone professional yet tinged with an undercurrent of urgency.

"Of course," Dr. Evans responded, her words crisp. "Let's get straight to it. You're here about the evidence from the Wilson case?"

"Exactly. We're hoping you've got something we can use." Brian's request was direct, his need for answers evident in his terse delivery.

Dr. Evans turned on her heel, leading the way to a secluded conference room. Its door swung open to reveal a long table, shrouded with evidence bags and tagged items. Detective Hayes and Officer Lee followed, their gazes fixing on the spread before them.

"Here's what we have," Dr. Evans announced, gesturing towards the collection of potential leads. She leaned over the table, her fingers hovering above each piece as if she could sense their secrets through the latex of her gloves.

She picked up a clear evidence bag, holding it aloft for the detectives to see. Inside, a shard of glass winked under the harsh fluorescent light. "From the car window," she stated. Her thumb traced the label attached to the bag, her focus absolute.

Next, her hand drifted to a cluster of fibers, each taped meticulously onto a white card. She tilted her head, studying the hues and textures with an intensity that bordered on reverence. "Could be from the upholstery," she murmured, almost to herself.

"Anything on them?" Brian asked, his voice low and expectant.

"Working on it," she replied without looking up. Her eyes scanned the evidence with clinical precision, no detail escaping her scrutiny.

"Keep us posted," Jessica added, her gaze matching Dr. Evans' for thoroughness.

"Always do." Dr. Evans gave a curt nod, already absorbed in the next piece of evidence—a soiled cloth that might just hold the DNA needed to crack the case wide open.

Detective Hayes leaned in, his eyes sharp as he studied the array of evidence. "Dr. Evans, your take on this?" His voice cut through the quiet buzz of the forensic lab.

"Initial thoughts—this glass shard," Dr. Evans began, her finger pausing over the bagged piece, "Its edges are clean, almost surgical. Indicates a break-in tool, not just brute force." Her observation hung in the air, a clue to the calculated nature of the crime.

"Precision. Planning," Hayes mused, his mind already sifting through suspect profiles.

"Exactly. And these fibers," she continued, pointing toward the collection on the card, "Not just from any upholstery. Preliminary comparison suggests high-end, custom-made. Possibly links our suspects to a specific auto shop or manufacturer."

"Good. What's our next step on those?" Hayes asked, his tone insistent.

"DNA testing on the cloth—hoping for skin cells. It's promising." Dr. Evans' eyes didn't waver from the task at hand. "The glass and fibers, we'll run through databases, check against known offenders." She was the calm center in a storm of questions, methodically plotting the path of their investigation.

"Timeframe?" Officer Lee chimed in, her pen poised above her notebook.

"Twenty-four hours for preliminary DNA results. Fingerprint analysis is underway, and fiber comparisons could take a bit longer," Dr. Evans replied, her words measured, betraying no hint of pressure despite the urgency hanging over them.

"Keep it tight, Laura. We're on the clock," Hayes said, acknowledging the race against time with a firm nod.

"Always do, Brian." Dr. Evans gave him a look that was all business, her confidence in her skills unspoken but unmistakable. She turned back to the evidence, ready to peel back layers of mystery with scientific precision.

Dr. Evans donned a pair of latex gloves with practiced ease, the snap of the material punctuating the silence of the conference room. She motioned for Detective Hayes and Officer Lee to do the same.

"Every contact leaves a trace," she stated, her voice the embodiment of focus as she handed them each a sterile swab kit. "We'll start by swabbing for additional DNA on the steering wheel and gearshift—areas likely to yield skin cells."

Hayes nodded, mirroring Dr. Evans' meticulous movements while swabbing the indicated areas. Officer Lee angled her head, watching intently, absorbing every detail of the procedure.

"Is there a chance the heat could've degraded any samples?" Lee asked, her eyes scanning the array of evidence spread before them.

"Degradation is always a concern," Dr. Evans admitted, her blue eyes locked onto the task at hand. "But our lab's equipped to handle it. We maximize what we can retrieve."

As they worked, Hayes held up a plastic bag containing a torn piece of checkered cloth, found in the trunk of the abandoned vehicle. "Could this be from a uniform? Maybe a diner or a mechanic's outfit?"

"Possible," Dr. Evans mused, taking the bag and holding it up to the light. "I'll compare it against known patterns and materials used in local businesses." Her fingers worked deftly, labeling another sample bag. "The nuances in the weave could tell us more about its origin."

"Footprints in the car—any leads there?" Hayes quizzed, his gaze sharp.

"Partial prints only. I'm running them through AFIS as we speak," she replied without missing a beat. "Shoe treads are next. We might get lucky with a match that could place our suspect at other scenes."

"Other scenes" echoed in the room, the weight of potential breakthroughs hanging in the air.

"Preservation's key," Dr. Evans reminded them, her calm demeanor a stark contrast to the urgency driving their actions. "We document everything before we move on to testing—photos, notes, the works. No stone unturned."

"Understood," Hayes said, his own resolve mirroring hers. He exchanged a glance with Lee, both aware of the gravity of their task. Every piece of evidence was a silent witness, waiting for its story to be told. They were determined to listen.

Dr. Evans flicked on the overhead light, illuminating the evidence sprawled across the table like a morbid jigsaw puzzle. "I've pieced together initial findings," she announced, her voice steady and commanding attention.

Detectives Hayes and Lee leaned in, their expressions taut with anticipation. Dr. Evans picked up a clear evidence bag containing a fragment of paper. "This," she said, pointing to the torn corner of a parking ticket, "was lodged in the driver's side door. It's dated the same day as the heist."

"Could place our suspect at the scene or nearby," Hayes muttered, his mind already racing through scenarios.

"Exactly," Dr. Evans confirmed. She moved to another item, a small, metallic shard. "And this is part of a key, likely snapped off in a struggle. I'm cross-referencing with locksmith databases."

"Any prints?" Lee inquired, her gaze sharp.

"Smudged, but I'm working on enhancing them." Dr. Evans' fingers danced over the items with practiced ease. She presented a plastic bag with a single hair follicle inside. "And here, we have a potential goldmine—a hair, root intact. DNA analysis is underway."

"Good work," Hayes said, the corners of his mouth lifting ever so slightly in appreciation.

"Let's not celebrate yet," Dr. Evans cautioned, her eyes still fixed on the evidence before her. She exuded focus, every fiber of her being dedicated to unearthing the truth hidden within these silent witnesses.

"Of course," Lee agreed, nodding solemnly. "But your insights are crucial. They shape where we go next."

"Happy to assist," Dr. Evans replied, though her tone suggested 'happy' was hardly the word. This was her mission, her purpose etched into every line of her face.

"Your expertise... It makes a difference, Laura," Hayes said, sincerity lacing his words. He met her piercing blue gaze, a silent acknowledgment passing between them.

"Thank you, Detective," she responded, her professional mask firmly in place. "Now, if you'll excuse me, there's more to be done."

Hayes and Lee exchanged a glance, an unspoken agreement that they were indeed in good hands. With a final nod of respect toward Dr. Evans, they turned to leave, their steps quickening with renewed urgency, ready to chase down the leads laid bare by science and tenacity.

"Remember, I'm just a call away," Dr. Evans said as she handed Detective Hayes a small stack of business cards. The fluorescent lights of the lab reflected off her glasses, casting an analytical glow over her features. "Anytime you need another run-through or if new evidence crops up, you know where to find me."

"Appreciated, Dr. Evans," Hayes replied, pocketing the cards. His gaze lingered on the meticulous layout of evidence that sprawled across the table, each piece a potential key to unlocking the case.

"Thanks, Laura," Officer Lee chimed in, her eyes tracing the path of their earlier discussion—fiber samples, fingerprints, the hair follicle. Each a breadcrumb on the trail to justice.

"Of course," Dr. Evans answered with a nod, her voice steady and assured. She began reorganizing the evidence with precise movements, restoring order to the chaos laid out before them.

The detectives turned toward the door, the weight of responsibility pressing on their shoulders. Their minds raced with the information shared, each detail a spark igniting the pathways of possibility.

"Let's move," Hayes said, determination etching his words. He led the way through the maze of sterile corridors, each step taking them closer to the streets where answers lay hidden.

Lee followed, her thoughts already sifting through the data, categorizing, analyzing. The forensic treasure trove they'd been privy to was a testament to Dr. Evans' skill and dedication—a beacon in the murky waters of criminal investigation.

They exited the lab, the city's sounds rushing to greet them. The air outside carried the scent of rain and asphalt—the scent of the city that held both the crime and its solution.

"Next stop, the canvas," Hayes stated, his mind on the witnesses that hadn't come forward, the eyes that had seen but remained silent.

"Every second counts now," Lee added, her stride matching Hayes'. They got into their unmarked car, the engine coming to life with a roar.

Hayes glanced at the rearview mirror, a reflection of a world waiting for justice. With Dr. Evans' findings burning bright in their arsenal, they drove off into the city's heart.

Chapter 5

Brian Hayes leaned over the cluttered desk, his blue eyes scanning the scattered files as if they were pieces of a jigsaw puzzle waiting to be connected. "What do we really know about Mike?" he asked, his voice echoing in the quiet office.

"Too little," Jessica Lee replied from across the table, her black hair tied back in a no-nonsense fashion. She tapped a pen against her notepad, a list of names and numbers already scribbled down. "We start digging into his past. Friends. Co-workers. Anyone who can fill in the blanks."

"Right." Brian nodded, picking up a photograph of Mike and Sheila together at a company event, their smiles too perfect. He set it down with a clack. "Let's split the list. You take the business partners, I'll handle the employees."

"Got it." Jessica stood, the determination in her eyes mirroring Brian's resolve.

They hit the pavement, questions loaded like rounds in a chamber. Time was their enemy now.

"Mike ever mention his wife or Sheila during poker night?" Brian's question cut through the smoky haze of a dimly-lit bar where one of Mike's acquaintances sipped on a bourbon.

"Marlene? Nah, man, it was all business with him," the contact drawled, eyes darting away.

"Business, huh?" Brian grunted, unconvinced. He scribbled a note before moving on.

Meanwhile, Jessica sat across from one of Mike's former employees in a sterile café, her posture alert. "Any gossip floating around the office about Mike? Anything about his personal life?"

The ex-employee stirred her coffee nervously. "Sheila? She's been around a lot. Always closed-door meetings, you know?"

"Meetings," Jessica echoed, her tone suggesting there was more to it than just work.

"Meetings," the woman confirmed, a hint of scandal in her voice. Jessica's pen flew across the page.

The afternoon waned as they canvassed for clues, the city's heartbeat pulsing around them. They reconvened in Brian's old Crown Vic, the dashboard littered with fast-food wrappers and stakeout remnants.

"Anything?" Brian asked, starting the ignition.

"Rumors about Sheila. Frequent 'meetings'. It's thin, but it's something," Jessica reported, her eyes weary yet sharp.

"Thin's better than nothing." Brian put the car in gear, pulling away from the curb. "Let's see how thin we can slice it."

Their investigation was gaining momentum, each question sharpening the blade that would cut to the heart of the matter. The truth was out there, and Brian and Jessica were determined to unearth it.

The witness leaned back in the cheap plastic chair, arms folded, a veneer of indifference failing to mask underlying anxiety. Brian studied him from across the narrow table, the fluorescent lights of the interrogation room casting harsh shadows across his face.

"Mike and Sheila," Brian began, his voice measured, "tell me about them."

A twitch at the corner of the witness's mouth betrayed nerves. "They were tight. Real close," he said, eyes flicking between Brian and Jessica.

"Close how?" Jessica pressed, notebook ready.

"Touchy. Whispery. Not just boss and worker, you know? More personal."

"Secretive glances?" Brian prodded.

"Like they had their own language." The witness shifted uncomfortably.

Brian exchanged a look with Jessica, the unspoken question hanging heavy between them: motive?

Jessica scribbled furiously, her brow furrowed. "Did Marlene know?"

"Everyone knew," the witness muttered, looking away.

"Everyone except Marlene?" Brian's tone sharpened.

"Maybe she did, maybe not. Who can keep up with what goes in that snake pit?"

"Thank you for your time," Jessica said, closing her notebook with finality.

Outside, the evening air was crisp, carrying the last golden hues of dusk. They walked to the car in silence, each lost in thought. As Brian unlocked the doors, Jessica turned to him, her expression grim.

"An affair is a classic motive," she said, breaking the silence. "If Marlene found out..."

"Then we need more than whispers and sideways looks," Brian countered, his jaw set. "Hard evidence."

"But you feel it too, don't you?" Jessica's gaze was searching. "Something's off with Mike."

"Feelings don't win cases," Brian said, but his gut churned with the same suspicion.

"Let's dig deeper," Jessica urged, determination etched into her features.

Brian nodded, the engine roaring to life beneath them. This was no longer just an investigation; it was a hunt. And they were closing in on their prey.

Brian flipped through the stack of phone records, his fingers pausing on a page marked with a series of red circles. "Look at this," he said, tapping the paper. "Calls between Mike and Sheila ramped up three weeks before Marlene's murder."

Jessica leaned over the desk, her ponytail brushing against her collar as she peered at the highlighted entries. "And texts," she added, her voice low and steady. "Late-night ones." She traced the lines connecting the dates and times, her brow creasing. "It's like they couldn't stay away from each other."

"Or were plotting something," Brian muttered, his blue eyes hardening.

The room was silent except for the hum of the fluorescent lights overhead. They sat side by side, surrounded by evidence that painted a damning picture—a timeline of clandestine communication.

"Surveillance footage next," Brian said, reaching for the remote. The screen flickered to life, showing grainy images of Mike and Sheila. Their interactions were professional at first glance, but the stolen touches, the lingering looks, betrayed more.

"Freeze it there." Jessica pointed to the corner of the screen where Sheila handed Mike what appeared to be a manila envelope. "Could be anything, but with them, I doubt it's innocent."

"Enough to get a warrant, you think?" Brian's question hung in the air, a gauntlet thrown down.

"More than enough." Jessica's reply was confident, her training evident in her decisive tone.

They moved quickly, efficiency born of urgency. The search warrant was signed off by a judge who knew Brian's reputation for thoroughness and Jessica's keen eye for detail.

"Let's go," Brian said, holstering his weapon as they headed out.

The search of Mike's office was methodical, each drawer and file scrutinized. Brian's experience and Jessica's diligence left no stone unturned. In the back of a filing cabinet, hidden beneath innocuous business contracts, Jessica found a batch of letters, their envelopes creased from handling.

"Got something," she called out, her heart racing as she unfolded the top letter. Her eyes scanned the looping handwriting—intimate words that confirmed their suspicions.

"Love letters," she said, passing them to Brian. His lips pressed into a thin line as he read, the confirmation of the affair almost palpable in his grasp.

"Check for prints," he instructed, his mind already cataloging the evidence.

Their search continued at Mike's house, where the personal nature of their investigation became even more intrusive. Photographs of Mike and Sheila, tucked away in a desk drawer, smirked up at them—images of secret rendezvous and shared smiles.

"Marlene never stood a chance," Jessica whispered, anger simmering beneath her professional veneer.

"Focus on the evidence," Brian reminded her, though his own gut twisted with distaste. "Emotions can wait."

The late hours ticked by as they bagged and tagged potential evidence. Finally, stepping out into the cool night, the weight of their findings heavy in their hands, Brian looked over at Jessica.

"Good work, Lee," he said, his voice betraying a hint of weariness. "But this is just the beginning."

"Ready for what comes next," she replied, her determination unwavering despite the darkness that edged closer with each piece of evidence.

Together, they drove back to the precinct, ready to piece together the puzzle of betrayal and murder that had ensnared them all.

Mike Thompson's office loomed ahead, a fortress of steel and glass that reflected the morning sun with blinding intensity. Inside, Brian and Jessica crossed the polished marble floor with purpose, their footsteps echoing like a countdown.

"Mr. Thompson, do you have a moment?" Brian's voice cut through the hum of activity as they entered Mike's office without waiting for an invitation.

Mike looked up from his mahogany desk, his eyes flickering with annoyance before settling into a practiced smile. "Detectives," he greeted them, rising to his full imposing height. "To what do I owe this pleasure?"

"Cut the pleasantries, Mike," Jessica said. Her tone was sharp, mirroring her gaze. "We need to talk about Sheila Chambers."

"Ah." Mike's smile didn't reach his eyes. He leaned back against his desk, arms folded. "Sheila is a valuable employee—nothing more."

"Phone records suggest otherwise," Brian interjected, watching Mike's face for any telltale slip. "You two were in constant contact, even late at night. Care to explain?"

"Business often requires after-hours attention," Mike replied smoothly. His hands remained steady, betraying no sign of guilt. "As for the nature of our communications, it remains strictly professional."

"Is that so?" Jessica challenged, stepping closer. "Because we found love letters, Mike. And photographs. Hardly professional."

Mike's facade wavered, just for a moment, but he recovered quickly. "Outlandish accusations based on circumstantial evidence," he scoffed. "I assure you, my relationship with Marlene was solid."

"Was it solid enough to withstand an affair?" Brian asked pointedly.

"Alleged affair," Mike corrected, his voice cool. "And no, Detective, it wouldn't be a motive for murder. You're barking up the wrong tree."

Jessica held his gaze, unflinching. "We'll see about that."

The detectives left Mike's office with the same briskness they had entered, exchanging a look that spoke volumes. They headed straight for the dealership where Sheila worked, the air between them charged with anticipation.

Sheila was perched on a high stool at the service counter when they arrived, her red hair a stark contrast against the sterile white walls. She eyed them with a mix of curiosity and defiance as they approached.

"Ms. Chambers, we need a word," Brian stated, flashing his badge.

"Regarding?" Sheila asked, sliding off the stool with an ease that belied her tension.

"Your relationship with Mike Thompson," Jessica said, getting straight to the point. "We know it was more than just professional."

"Accusations require proof," Sheila retorted, crossing her arms. "And I have nothing to hide."

"Even from Marlene?" Brian pressed.

Sheila's posture stiffened. "Marlene's death was a tragedy, but it has nothing to do with me."

"Except for the fact that you were sleeping with her husband," Jessica pointed out.

"Consensual adults are entitled to privacy," Sheila fired back, her eyes narrowing. "Our personal lives are not on trial here."

"Maybe," Brian conceded, watching her closely, "but if your personal life intersects with a murder investigation, that privacy becomes a lot less certain."

"Are you charging me with something?" Sheila's voice was steady, but there was a glint of worry behind her green eyes.

"Not yet," Jessica replied. "But we're far from done, Sheila."

Leaving the dealership, Brian and Jessica shared a silent agreement. The confrontation had only deepened their resolve. They would unravel this web of lies, one thread at a time.

The low hum of the precinct's fluorescent lights served as a persistent backdrop to Brian's focus. He spread out the photos on his desk, one depicting Mike and Sheila at a company event, their proximity less than professional. But it was the grainy still from a surveillance camera that truly piqued Jessica's interest as she leaned over his shoulder.

"Got something?" her voice cut through the tense air.

"Look at this," Brian pointed, "timestamped the morning of Marlene's murder." The black-and-white image showed Mike and Sheila outside a convenience store, mere blocks from Marlene's house. Their stances—too close, faces drawn in heated exchange—spoke volumes.

"Coincidence?" Jessica asked, skepticism lacing her tone.

"Too convenient. They argued in public; who knows what went down in private?"

"Right before Marlene died..." Jessica's words trailed off, her mind racing with implications.

Brian's eyes were hard as flint. "We need more. If they're involved..."

"DNA would tie them to the scene," Jessica interjected, her brain already sifting through procedures for obtaining samples. "It's a long shot."

"Long shots are better than no shots." Brian's resolve was palpable. "Let's talk strategy." They huddled closer, plotting their next move in the dance of evidence and suspicion.

Brian hovered near the dealership's coffee machine, feigning nonchalance. Cups clinked and steam hissed as he seized the moment Sheila discarded her Styrofoam cup, the lipstick stain a silent witness. With a practiced sleight of hand, the cup disappeared into a plastic evidence bag.

"Got it," he murmured into his mic.

"Copy that," Jessica's voice crackled in his earpiece. She was across town, outside Mike's favorite gym, eyes sharp for an opportunity. It came when Mike tossed his water bottle into a public trashcan before disappearing into his polished sedan. Jessica darted forward, retrieving the bottle with a swift gesture, sealing it away from contamination.

"Sample secured," she confirmed, satisfaction seeping through the static.

"Let's get these to the lab," Brian said, already en route to their rendezvous.

***

The wait was a drawn-out agony, each tick of the clock stretching seconds into hours. Brian paced while Jessica sat, her leg bouncing with pent-up energy. Then the call came, slicing through the tension like a blade.

"Detective Hayes? We've processed the samples," the lab technician's voice was clinical, detached. "You'll want to see this."

"Go ahead," Brian braced himself on his desk.

"Female DNA found at the crime scene is a match to the sample you provided. Sheila Chambers' DNA is all over it."

A charged silence fell upon them. Breakthrough.

"Thank you," Brian managed, his mind already catapulting into what came next.

Jessica's eyes met his, a mirror of his own resolve. They had her. Now the real work began.

Chapter 6

Detective Brian Hayes flicked through the case files, his salt-and-pepper hair casting shifting shadows in the lamplight. He exhaled sharply, a sound of frustration that Officer Jessica Lee knew all too well by now. She leaned in across the desk, her ponytail brushing against the scattered papers as she studied the photographs and notes they had amassed on Marlene's murder.

"Another dead end," Brian muttered, closing the folder with a definitive thud. His piercing blue eyes met Jessica's, a silent commiseration passing between them.

Jessica straightened, tapping a pen against the edge of the desk. "We're missing something," she said. "There has to be another angle we haven't considered."

Brian nodded, rubbing at the stubble lining his jaw. "Mike's alibi—it's solid?"

"Seems so," Jessica replied, her voice laced with reluctance. "But what if—just what if—he's telling the truth?"

"Then we're back to square one." He stared at the board pinned with strings and photographs. "Let's retrace our steps. Who else had a motive?"

"Marlene's ex? The neighbor with the noise complaints?" she suggested, her brown eyes narrowing as she pondered the possibilities.

"Too easy," Brian countered, his mind racing. "What about her work? Any disgruntled clients or colleagues?"

"Could be worth looking into," Jessica conceded, jotting down the idea.

"Okay, let's dig deeper there," he decided. "Tomorrow we hit the ground running. Fresh eyes might spot what we've been missing."

"Got it," Jessica affirmed, her determination unwavering. They stood together, surrounded by the remnants of their stalled investigation, the urgent, investigative tone hanging heavy in the air—a challenge they were determined to meet head-on.

The sun glared down on the lot, a sea of gleaming metal and price tags. Brian Hayes squinted against the brightness as he and Jessica Lee approached Mike Thompson's domain: Thompson's Pre-Owned Motors. The scent of hot asphalt mixed with car wax wafted in the air.

"Remember, we're just fact-finding," Brian murmured, scanning the dealership for signs of life beyond the rows of vehicles.

"Understood," Jessica replied, her ponytail bouncing as she nodded.

They entered the showroom, the chime of the door slicing through the hum of conversation. A salesman glanced up, his smile faltering at the sight of the badges clipped to their belts.

"Can we help you?" he asked, masking his unease with a well-practiced grin.

"Detective Hayes, Officer Lee. We need to speak with the staff about Mike Thompson," Brian stated, bypassing the pleasantries.

"Is Mike in some kind of trouble?" the salesman ventured, attempting to maintain his composure.

"Just routine questions," Jessica interjected before Brian could reply. She caught the quick exchange of looks between two other employees. "We'll start with you."

The salesman straightened, clearing his throat. "Mike was here the night of the murder. Late deal." His words came too quickly, rehearsed.

"Anyone else can confirm that?" Brian's voice was flat, his gaze unwavering.

"Ted, over there. He closed up with him," came the response, a finger pointed toward a man shuffling papers at a desk.

Brian nodded to Jessica, who made her way to Ted while Brian continued his interrogation. "Notice anything unusual about Mike that night?"

"Unusual?" The salesman hesitated, weighing his answer. "No. Just... focused, I guess."

"Focused on what?" Brian prodded.

"Work, you know? Deals, paperwork."

Jessica returned, her expression telling. "Ted confirms it, but something's off. Hesitant."

"Let's talk to everyone, get a full picture," Brian decided, signaling for her to follow.

They moved from one employee to another, each question sharp and direct; each answer dissected for truth or hesitation. Some confirmed Mike's alibi without missing a beat, others stumbled over details, eyes darting away.

"Patterns emerging," Jessica whispered to Brian as they regrouped. "Some sure, others not so much."

"Coached versus genuine," Brian concluded. He checked his watch. "Let's wrap this up."

"Anything else you remember about that night?" Jessica asked the group, her voice carrying across the room.

Silence, then a mechanic spoke up. "Mike, he was anxious. Kept checking his watch."

"Anxious about a sale?" Brian questioned.

"Maybe," the mechanic shrugged. "Just seemed more on edge than usual."

"Thanks," Brian said, his mind already racing with this new sliver of information.

"Let's go," he motioned to Jessica, stepping out of the dealership. They left behind a ripple of whispers, the air thick with suspicion and hints of fear.

"Next steps?" Jessica asked as they reached the car.

"Cross-reference time stamps with security footage, if they have any," Brian replied, starting the engine. "And keep digging. Something doesn't sit right."

"Got it," Jessica affirmed, her gaze locked on the rearview mirror, the image of the dealership growing smaller but no less significant.

The car's interior was silent, save for the scratch of pen on paper as Jessica jotted down notes. Brian drummed his fingers on the steering wheel—each tap a ticking clock in their search for truth. The dealership faded into the distance, its secrets momentarily out of reach.

"Anything?" Brian asked, glancing over at Jessica.

"Still piecing it together—" Her words cut short by the chirp of her phone. A text message flashed on the screen. Unknown number. Jessica's brow furrowed as she read aloud.

"Mike might've bought himself an alibi."

Brian's fingers stilled. "Source?"

"Anonymous," she said, eyes narrowing.

"Could be a trap," he mused, eyes back on the road.

"Or a lead." Her voice carried a hopeful edge.

"Let's see where it takes us."

Minutes later, they were back at the precinct, diving through records and making calls. Leads chased like shadows—elusive, yet persistent. Each interview, another thread to untangle the web of deceit they suspected Mike had spun.

"Remember anyone unusual around Mike that night?" Jessica pressed an employee over the phone, her tone insistent but measured.

"Think, think..." The voice on the other end trailed off, then snapped back. "Yeah, there was this guy. Didn't know him. Mike kept him close."

"Description?" Brian interjected, hovering nearby.

"Average build. Brown jacket. Nervous tick with his left eye."

"Name?" Jessica pushed.

"Never caught it."

"Thanks," Brian said, ending the call. He met Jessica's gaze. "That's something."

"Could match the tip," Jessica added, her pulse quickening with the thrill of the chase.

"Let's find this mystery man," Brian decided, the hunt reigniting the fire within. "See if Mike's generosity extends beyond discounts on sedans."

They split up, canvassing contacts and informants, digging through databases for men matching the description. Time slipped by unheeded as they worked, relentless, determined. This was more than just a lead—it was a crack in Mike Thompson's carefully crafted façade.

"Got a hit," Jessica called out across the room, her eyes glued to the computer screen.

"Talk to me," Brian said, moving to her side.

"Surveillance footage from a bar two blocks from the dealership. Night of the murder. There's our guy—brown jacket, nervous tick."

"Alone?" Brian questioned.

"Wait for it..." She clicked through the frames. "And there's Mike. Handshake. Exchange."

"Payment for silence?" Brian's voice was a low growl.

"Looks like it." Jessica's fingers flew over the keyboard, enhancing the image. "We need to bring him in."

"Let's move." Brian was already on his feet, the urgency palpable.

Together they stepped out, the air crisp with anticipation. The truth was close, and they were ready to seize it.

The clock on the dashboard read 11:03 PM as Brian Hayes steered the unmarked sedan into the dimly lit parking lot. Beside him, Jessica Lee checked her notes, her brow furrowed in concentration.

"This is it," Brian said, killing the engine. "The place Mike swore he was all night."

"Let's see if the story holds up." Jessica's voice held an edge of skepticism. They stepped out into the chill night air, the neon sign of the pool hall buzzing softly above them.

Inside, the clack of billiard balls and the murmur of conversation greeted them. Brian scanned the room, his eyes adapting to the haze of cigarette smoke and dim lighting. Jessica approached the bar, badge at the ready.

"We need to talk about the night Marlene was killed," she said to the bartender, a burly man with a no-nonsense look.

"Police, huh?" He wiped his hands on a rag, eyeing them warily. "Mike Thompson? Yeah, he was here."

"Can you confirm that for the entire night?" Brian joined her, his gaze steady.

"Most of it. Took off early though, said he wasn't feeling well." The bartender shrugged, then paused. "But there was something off about him."

"Off how?" Jessica leaned in, sensing the shift.

"Kept checking his phone, antsy like. Left around when the news broke about the murder." The bartender tapped his fingers on the counter. "Said he was going home, but he headed west. Home's east."

Brian and Jessica exchanged a glance. West led back to the dealership—back to the scene.

"Anyone else notice this?" Brian asked, trying to keep his voice level despite the adrenaline spiking through his veins.

"Ask Lenny," the bartender nodded towards a corner booth. "Plays here most nights, sharp memory."

They found Lenny, an elderly man with hawkish eyes, lining up a shot. At their approach, he straightened, assessing them with a shrewd gaze.

"Detectives," he acknowledged, having recognized the telltale signs of law enforcement. "About Mike?"

"Did you see him leave that night?" Jessica questioned, her tone direct.

"Sure did. Wasn't his usual self. Seemed in a hurry to get somewhere." Lenny chalked his cue stick, not missing a beat. "Trouble is, he left his coat. When I went to return it, caught a glimpse of him arguing with some fella outside. Didn't look like any car buyer to me."

"Could you describe the man?" Brian asked, his mind racing with the implications.

"Average height, stocky build. Wore a leather jacket. They were heated, and Mike looked mighty stressed," Lenny recounted.

"Thank you, Lenny," Jessica said, her thoughts already turning over this new piece of evidence.

"Looks like Mike's alibi isn't as solid as we thought," Brian murmured as they walked back to the car. "We've got work to do."

"Let's pull those tapes from the area," Jessica suggested, her eyes reflecting the glow of determination. "See what they're hiding."

"Agreed." Brian started the car, the engine humming to life. "It's unraveling, Jess. Whatever facade Mike's put up, it's starting to crack."

As they drove off, the pool hall fading into the night behind them, neither spoke. The truth was out there, and they were inching closer. The hunt was on, and every second counted.

The dealership's fluorescent lights cast long shadows as Brian and Jessica approached Mike Thompson, who was leaning casually against a sleek sedan, his salesman smile in place.

"Mike," Brian began, voice steady, "we need to talk."

"Detective Hayes, Officer Lee," Mike greeted, straightening up. "To what do I owe the pleasure?"

"Your alibi," Jessica said without preamble, her gaze fixed on him. "It's got holes."

Mike's smile faltered, just a twitch at the corner of his mouth, but he recovered quickly. "I'm not sure what you mean. I've been nothing but cooperative."

"Cooperative people don't argue with mysterious men outside pool halls when they're supposed to be selling cars," Brian countered.

Mike's eyes narrowed imperceptibly. "That could have been any night. People come and go, disagreements happen."

"Not the night of Marlene's murder," Jessica pushed. "That night you were seen, Mike. And not here."

"Is that so?" Mike's tone remained smooth, but his jaw clenched.

"Care to explain?" Brian asked.

"Nothing to explain," Mike replied, his composure a mask that didn't quite reach his eyes.

"Right." Brian's voice was dry. "We'll see about that."

They left Mike standing there, his charm ineffective, the air charged with unspoken threats.

Back at the precinct, Brian rapped on the doorframe of Captain Reynolds' office.

"Got a minute, Cap?" Brian asked as he and Jessica stepped in.

"Always for you two. What's up?" Reynolds looked up from his paperwork, his seasoned eyes sharp.

"We've found inconsistencies in Mike Thompson's alibi," Jessica explained. "Witness places him away from the dealership on the night of the murder."

"Means motive, opportunity," Brian added. "We think it's time to dig deeper."

"Surveillance? Search warrant?" Reynolds surmised, leaning back in his chair.

"Both, if we can swing it," Brian said. "We need to see what he's hiding."

"Alright," Reynolds nodded, reaching for his phone. "I'll talk to the DA. You two put together your evidence for the warrant request. We'll need to make it stick."

"Will do, Cap," Jessica affirmed, already mentally cataloging the evidence.

"Good work," Reynolds said, watching them leave. "Bring me something solid."

Brian and Jessica shared a look, determination etched into their features. It was game time, and they were ready to play.

The clock ticked ominously in the background as Brian shuffled through the stack of affidavits and statements, his eyes scanning for any overlooked detail that could crack the case wide open. Jessica hovered nearby, phone pressed to her ear, her voice a mix of persuasion and frustration as she attempted to coax more information from reluctant witnesses.

"Listen, I just need you to confirm what you saw," she urged, the receiver capturing the tremble of urgency in her tone.

Brian glanced over, catching the slight shake of her head. No luck. He turned back to the papers, the words blurring into a jumble of useless ink. They needed something, anything that would give them leverage, but the legal system was a labyrinth they couldn't navigate without more evidence.

"Another dead end," Jessica said, hanging up with a sigh. "They won't talk without a lawyer present, and even then, they're spooked."

"Dammit," Brian muttered under his breath. His mind raced, trying to piece together an alternative route they could take. They had been so sure that pressing Mike would yield results, but he was slippery, a master at maintaining his facade.

"DA's hands are tied too," Brian grumbled, remembering Reynolds' earlier call. "Without concrete evidence, no judge will sign off on a search warrant."

Jessica's brow furrowed, her youthful optimism warring with the harsh reality of their situation. "So, what now? We can't let this guy walk."

Brian leaned heavily against the desk, feeling the weight of years and unsolved cases bearing down on him. His blue eyes met hers, silently conveying the shared burden of their duty. "We keep digging," he said, though the fire behind his words was dimming.

"Every angle has been played out," Jessica countered, her ponytail swishing as she turned to face him, her eyes alight with a different kind of fire—one that refused to be extinguished. "We need a new angle, something we haven't seen."

"Or someone who hasn't been scared silent yet," Brian added, though the prospect seemed increasingly unlikely.

"Let's go over it all again," Jessica suggested, determination lacing her voice. Her fingers drummed against the desk, the rhythm syncing with Brian's own restless energy.

"Again," Brian echoed. The two of them plunged back into the files, combing through the records with the hope that something had been missed. Hours slipped by, unnoticed, until the office was cloaked in shadows cast by the dying light.

No revelation came. The stubborn silence of the paper echoed the silence of their leads—empty and unyielding. They were stuck, motionless in a current that should have swept them forward.

"Another day tomorrow," Jessica said finally, her voice a mere whisper in the quiet room. The usual spark in her eyes was dimmed by the shadow of defeat.

"Tomorrow," Brian confirmed, but the word tasted bitter. They packed up, the heaviness of their frustration a tangible presence between them. As they left the precinct, the night air did nothing to ease the stifling sense of being trapped in a maze with no exit.

They needed a breakthrough, but as the city lights blinked mockingly at them, both knew that elusive leads might just as well be mirages—visible but forever out of reach.

Chapter 7

Sam Miller flitted between the racks of colorful costumes with the grace of a seasoned performer, his shaggy blond hair bouncing with each enthusiastic step. Theatrical posters adorned the walls of the costume shop, each one a siren call to the world he adored. He adjusted his glasses and beamed at a customer hesitating between a pirate outfit and a Renaissance gown.

"Think swashbuckling adventure on the high seas or the elegance of courtly intrigue," Sam suggested, gesturing grandly as if on stage. "Which story would you rather live out?"

The customer laughed, caught up in Sam's fervor, her indecision swept away by his passion for storytelling through attire.

"Let's go with the pirate," she decided, her eyes reflecting the thrill of an imagined escapade.

"Excellent choice!" Sam exclaimed. He wrapped the costume with care, his movements quick, practiced.

As the bell above the door chimed, Sam glanced up. A familiar figure entered, red hair ablaze against the backdrop of feather boas and sequined masks. Sheila Chambers. His brow furrowed subtly as he watched her stride purposefully toward the clown costumes, her piercing green eyes scanning the selection with intent.

He knew that face, had seen it before—a face not easily forgotten. Curiosity prickled at him. Why clowns? He tucked the question away like a script line to be delivered at the right moment.

"Anything else I can help you find today?" Sam asked the pirate-bound customer, handing over the neatly bagged costume. His voice was warm, but his gaze remained fixed on Sheila as she fingered a garish purple wig.

"Got everything, thanks," the customer replied, oblivious to the tension weaving itself through the store's narrow aisles.

"Break a leg," Sam called after her, the theater kid's farewell, before turning his full attention to the enigma wrapped in a scarlet coat exploring the realm of painted smiles and exaggerated laughter.

Sam's pulse quickened. Sheila Chambers, the woman now scrutinizing a rack of clown costumes, wasn't just another customer. It hit him—the local news story from last week, a robbery by someone in a clown outfit. He remembered bagging that very costume; her piercing green eyes had flicked up to his as she paid in cash.

"Can I help you find anything?" Sam asked, his voice steady though his mind raced. She turned, her gaze sharp and assessing.

"Thanks, I'm just browsing," Sheila replied with an air of nonchalance.

"Of course," Sam nodded, watching as she slid a polka-dotted tie back onto the display. He memorized her movements, the tilt of her head, the way she dismissed certain costumes. Details mattered.

The bell over the door jangled again, pulling Sam from his surveillance. Two figures entered, their bearing official—Detective Brian Hayes and Officer Jessica Lee. Sam's stomach fluttered with nervous anticipation. This was it.

"Good afternoon," Brian greeted, his blue eyes scanning the shop before settling on Sam. "We're here about the robbery last Thursday."

"Sam Miller," Sam extended a hand, feeling the weight of the moment. "I might have something for you."

Jessica stepped forward, her brown eyes alert. "Oh?"

"Clown costume. The woman there," Sam gestured subtly towards Sheila, "she bought one last week. I remember her—red hair, green eyes... unforgettable."

"Did you notice anything unusual about her behavior?" Brian's voice was direct, cutting to the chase.

"Paid in cash," Sam recalled, "and seemed... precise. Like she knew exactly what she wanted."

"Thank you, Mr. Miller. That's very helpful," Jessica said, jotting down notes.

"Anything else I can do," Sam offered, "just say the word."

"Actually," Brian began, "we might need to look at your sales records. And any surveillance footage you have."

"Sure thing, follow me." Sam led them to the counter, feeling the gravity of each step. His identification of Sheila could change everything.

Sam leaned against the counter, his gaze steady as he addressed Detective Hayes. "She walked in with purpose," he began, the memory vivid in his mind. "Red hair, striking against a black leather jacket. Green eyes, sharp, scanning the clown costumes."

"Did she say anything?" Brian asked, pen poised over his notepad.

"Minimal." Sam tapped his temple, signaling his recollection. "Asked for size options, checked the stitching, quality... like she was planning something big."

"Anything else stand out to you about her?" Officer Lee interjected, her tone indicating the importance of even the smallest detail.

"Her hands," Sam said quickly. "No hesitation. She picked up a frilly collar, a red nose, and the wig—fire-engine red to match her own hair. Odd choice if you're trying to blend in."

"Or send a message," Brian muttered, his expression hardening.

"Exactly." Sam nodded, pleased with his contribution. "Confident. That's how I'd describe her. Like she's done this before."

"Thank you, Sam," Jessica said warmly, her gratitude evident. "You have a good eye. It's been instrumental."

"Detail is key in theater," Sam replied with a half-smile, his nerves settling into a quiet pride.

"Let's move on it," Brian said to Jessica, urgency infusing his voice. "She's our lead now. We need to find out what that message was."

"Absolutely," Jessica agreed, her posture shifting to one ready for action. "Your help could crack this wide open."

As they turned to leave, Sam felt a flicker of excitement—his love for detail had just become part of something much bigger than any stage he'd ever known.

Brian's eyes flicked to the store's corners, searching out cameras. "We'll need the surveillance footage. Confirm it was her."

"First thing," Jessica affirmed, scribbling a note.

"Then we bring her in," Brian continued, his voice clipped with resolve. "Question her with what we've got."

"Let's hope she slips up," Jessica said, her lips tightening.

"Or just confesses." Brian's chuckle was devoid of humor.

Sam stood by, his chest tight. This was real. His information wasn't just useful; it was pivotal. He watched as the detectives made their way toward the exit, their strides purposeful. The bell above the door jingled as they left, slicing through the shop's quiet.

He lingered there, fingers tracing the counter's edge. Excitement bubbled inside him, laced with an edge of fear. Could his words really tip the scales? Sam swallowed hard, feeling the weight of his testimony. His glance darted to the door, where the detectives had disappeared into the world beyond—a world that now contained the consequences of his actions.

The hard drive whirred as Detective Brian Hayes pressed play. Beside him, Officer Jessica Lee leaned forward, her eyes locked onto the grainy images flickering across the computer screen. The footage from the costume shop's security cameras offered a silent narrative, one that might just speak volumes in the case they were tearing into.

"Pause there," Jessica said sharply, tapping a finger on the monitor. "That's her. That's got to be Sheila Chambers."

Brian squinted, studying the woman in the video dressed in a vivid red coat, her green eyes scanning the aisle of clown costumes. The timestamp corroborated Sam Miller's detailed account. She moved with purpose, as if aware of the camera but indifferent to its silent gaze.

"Same build. Same hair," Brian muttered, making notes. "Sam's description is spot on."

"Look at her demeanor," Jessica pointed out. "Confident. Too confident?"

"Maybe. But confidence doesn't make her guilty." Brian's fingers drummed on the desk. Evidence—that's what they needed.

"Her posture, though. It's like she's casing the place, not shopping," Jessica observed.

"Let's get everything we can from this footage. We need a full picture before we bring her in." Brian's voice was steady, his resolve clear.

"Agreed." Jessica nodded, jotting down their next steps.

They watched Sheila select the clown outfit, the transaction unfolding. No hesitation in her movements, no second-guessing. She paid in cash—another note for the detectives—a preference for anonymity?

"Sam's memory is a gift," Jessica remarked. "Without him, we'd have less to go on."

"Let's use it then. We'll prep for the interview. Go over what we know, play it out." Brian stood up, stretching his back. "Sheila Chambers won't see us coming."

"Right. We approach her with the evidence, keep it tight. No room for slip-ups." Jessica gathered the papers, her eyes sharp and focused. "We've got one shot to get her to talk."

"Exactly. We'll keep it close to the vest. If she's behind this, she's smart. We need to be smarter."

"Let's do it."

"First thing tomorrow," Brian confirmed, his mind already racing through possible interrogation tactics.

"Tomorrow," Jessica echoed, a determined glint in her eye.

They shut down the computer, the click echoing in the silence. The footage, now copied and safely stored, was their ace in the hole—their path to the truth. The detectives left the room, each step charged with the urgency of the hunt. Tomorrow they would face Sheila Chambers. And they would be ready.

The sun was already high in the sky as Detective Brian Hayes and Officer Jessica Lee stepped out of their unmarked car, the glare bouncing off the chrome bumpers of repossessed vehicles lining Mike's car dealership. The lot was a jungle of metal and ambition, and at its heart prowled Sheila Chambers.

"Ready?" Brian asked, his eyes scanning for the fiery red that would mark their suspect.

"Let's do this," Jessica replied curtly, her hand resting on the notepad in her pocket. They moved in unison, badges concealed, purpose etched into every step.

The air buzzed with the hum of engines being tested and the distant chatter of negotiations. It was thick with tension, anticipation wrapping around them like a second skin. Every step forward tightened the invisible thread pulling them towards Sheila.

They spotted her then, the red hair unmistakable even from a distance, her posture radiating control as she circled a sleek sedan like a hawk eyeing prey. She was mid-conversation with a customer, her gestures confident, her laugh devoid of warmth.

"Showtime," muttered Jessica, her pulse a steady drumbeat against the adrenaline coursing through her veins.

Brian nodded, feeling the weight of the evidence in his pocket—an anchor of certainty. They approached, weaving through the maze of cars, each one a silent witness to the impending confrontation.

"Ms. Chambers?" Brian called out, his voice carrying over the lot.

Sheila turned, her green eyes sharp, calculating the interruption. Her smile didn't reach those eyes, a predator's gaze assessing the situation.

"Detective Hayes, Officer Lee," she greeted, her tone measured, betraying nothing. "To what do I owe the pleasure?"

Jessica felt the moment teeter, a seesaw of power about to tip. "We have a few questions for you."

"Here?" Sheila's eyebrow arched, her composure a fortress.

"Preferably somewhere private," Brian insisted, his stance firm.

She considered them for a beat, the silence stretching taut. Then she nodded, excusing herself from the customer with a charm that didn't quite disguise the steel underneath.

"Follow me," she said, leading them toward the dealership office, her steps never faltering.

The detectives shared a glance, their resolve mirrored in each other's eyes. This was it—the pivotal moment where secrets would begin to unravel, where their investigation could either tighten or fray.

As they entered the office, the door closed behind them with a click that sounded far too much like the cocking of a gun. Sheila took a seat, her back straight, her face an unreadable mask.

"Detectives?" she prompted, as if inviting them to begin a game she had no intention of losing.

Brian and Jessica exchanged a nod, and as Brian pulled out the folded printout of the surveillance footage, the chapter ended, leaving readers hanging on the precipice of revelation. What would Sheila's reaction be? Would she crumble under the weight of evidence, or would she wield her cunning to slip through yet another crack?

Chapter 8

The case was at a standstill. Weeks of investigation had yielded little more than circumstantial connections and hunches—nothing concrete to pin Sheila Chambers to the murder. The cunning repossessor's alibi had checked out, and interviews circled back to dead ends. Sheila's red hair and green eyes were imprinted on every detective's mind, yet evidence remained as elusive as her demeanor.

Dr. Laura Evans approached the abandoned getaway car, a steely resolve in her blue eyes. She snapped on her latex gloves with practiced ease, the sound slicing through the quiet of the impound lot. Every inch of the vehicle would tell its story to her; all it required was her unwavering focus.

Laura started at the driver's seat, her movements deliberate. She dusted for fingerprints, the brush strokes gentle against the wheel. No detail escaped her—the position of the mirrors, the angle of the seat, the faint impressions on the pedals. Each observation was catalogued mentally, ready to be cross-checked against known facts.

She slid into the cramped backseat, the space telling of haste and perhaps recklessness. With fine-tipped tweezers and a magnifying glass, she scoured the upholstery. Fibers, fragments, anything that shouldn't be there—Laura sought the silent witnesses to the crime.

Methodical and meticulous, she moved through the car like a surgeon in the operating room. Each compartment opened, each surface swabbed. In the world of forensics, Dr. Evans was relentless, her expertise a beacon in the dim landscape of uncertainty.

The trunk was next. She lifted the lid, the hydraulic hinges giving way without complaint. The stark interior held the potential of secrets untold. Laura leaned in, her senses heightened, scouring for the shred of evidence that could unravel Sheila's tightly woven narrative.

In the face of frustration, where leads had run dry and hope was threadbare, Dr. Laura Evans worked with a calm urgency. Every fiber of her being was dedicated to the truth, to finding the missing piece that would speak when suspects stayed silent. And in this abandoned car, under her scrupulous gaze, that truth was waiting to be found.

Laura's eyes narrowed, a glint of blue ice fixated on the floor mat. Amidst the dull fibers, a strand of vibrant orange mocked the monochrome scene—a stark contrast to the muted grays and blacks. It was too deliberate, too vivid to belong.

"Got you," she whispered under her breath.

With the delicate precision of an archivist handling ancient manuscripts, Laura deployed her tweezers. The orange wig fiber surrendered easily, lifted from its hiding place. She didn't stop there. Her gaze swept across the expanse of the car's interior, hungry for more.

In the driver's seat, nestled between the seams where fabric met leather, another discovery lay in wait. Strands of red—distinctive, unmistakable. Sheila's signature hair, strands that matched the fiery hue depicted in countless witness descriptions.

Each strand, a silent accusation; each fiber, a subtle nod to guilt.

Laura's hands were steady. This was her domain—the pursuit of justice through the microscopic battlefield of evidence. She plucked the strands, one by one, ensuring no cross-contamination. The integrity of the samples was paramount.

"Into the bag you go," she murmured, placing them with care into separate evidence sachets labeled with meticulous handwriting. Dr. Evans did not believe in coincidence, not in her line of work. Each piece of evidence was a voice in the choir, building towards a crescendo of truth.

Sealing the sachets, Laura knew the narrative was shifting. These tiny witnesses, once part of a disguise and a person, now held the power to link Sheila to a crime that had gripped the city in a chokehold of fear. They were the silent sentinels, ready to speak volumes in a court of law, ready to betray the cunning of a woman who thought she could outsmart the system.

The samples secured, Laura allowed herself a rare moment of satisfaction. This was progress, tangible and undeniable. But there was no time to bask in the potential breakthrough; the clock was ticking, and every second mattered.

"Evans to Hayes," she clipped into her recorder, "possible match on the wig fibers and hair samples. We need to talk."

Laura Evans' fingers danced over her phone, the screen illuminating her determined gaze. "Hayes. Lee. Lab. Now," she texted, her message as crisp as her starched lab coat. The ticking of the wall clock punctuated the silence, its steady rhythm mirroring her quickening pulse. Every second mattered.

The crime lab was a symphony of beeps and hums by the time Detective Brian Hayes and Officer Jessica Lee arrived. Laura's back was a rigid line of anticipation as she faced the gleaming microscope, the evidence displayed like a dealer's hand on the table beside her.

"Found these in the getaway car," she announced without preamble, pointing to the wig fibers and hair strands neatly encased in plastic. Her finger hovered above them, not touching, but emphasizing their importance. The air in the room seemed to still, every eye locked onto the tiny, but potentially condemning, threads of evidence.

"Orange wig fibers, identical to the clown costume," Laura continued, her voice stripped of any inflection that wasn't strictly professional. She handed over latex gloves before presenting the sachets for closer inspection. "And these," she said, directing their attention to the strands of dark hair, "match Sheila's."

Brian leaned in, his seasoned eyes scanning the samples, while Jessica absorbed every detail, her mind clearly racing through the implications. The fluorescent lights cast an unforgiving glare on the scene, highlighting the gravity etched into their faces.

"Could be the link we needed," Laura stated, though she left no room for premature celebration. There was work to be done, analysis to confirm, a case to build. But this was a start—a solid, indisputable start—and in the world of criminal investigation, that was a flicker of hope in the dark expanse of uncertainty.

Detective Hayes squinted at the evidence, his fingers brushing over the plastic as if he could will it to yield more answers. "She wore the clown costume," he murmured, almost to himself. Beside him, Officer Lee nodded, her posture rigid with tension.

"Sure looks like it," she replied, her voice barely above a whisper. "But it's circumstantial, isn't it?"

"Without a doubt." Hayes straightened up, the lines in his face deepening. He turned to face Lee, his blue eyes sharp and focused. "Fibers and hair don't place her at Marlene's house. They don't put the weapon in her hand."

Lee's lips pressed into a thin line. "We know she was involved. But proving it..."

"Proving it is another beast altogether." Frustration simmered in Hayes' tone. In his decades on the force, he'd seen plenty of cases slip through the cracks. Evidence that hinted, suggested, implied—but never quite sealed the deal.

"Damning," Lee echoed his earlier thought, her gaze lingering on the samples. "But not enough."

"Exactly." Hayes exhaled sharply, a gust of disappointment fogging the air between them. "We need something solid. Irrefutable."

"Something to directly connect Sheila to Marlene's murder," Lee concluded, her determination flaring despite the setback. Hayes saw it in her eyes—the same fire that had driven him all these years. It was the kind of passion that solved cases, the relentless pursuit of truth.

"Back to square one," Hayes said, though his voice held no defeat. Just a hardened resolve. "We keep digging."

Lee nodded, her ponytail swaying with the motion. Together, they stood amid the stark white of the lab, surrounded by the silent promise of justice yet to be fulfilled. The case was far from closed, the path to conviction obscured, but neither of them would rest until every avenue was explored.

The fluorescent lights cast a harsh glow over the cluttered conference table, revealing pages of notes and crime scene photos splayed out like a macabre deck of cards. Detective Brian Hayes leaned forward, his eyes scanning the array of evidence with a predator's intensity. Officer Jessica Lee mirrored his posture, her pen tapping a rapid, silent drumbeat on the tabletop.

"Okay," Hayes began, voice low and steady, "we need a new angle—anything that'll stick."

Lee's nod was quick, decisive. "Witnesses? Security cams? There's got to be something we missed."

"Revisit the timeline," Hayes suggested. "Sheila's alibi, her whereabouts before and after the murder. There must be a crack."

"Neighbors," Lee said, snatching up a notepad. "Let's press them again. Someone might have seen her leaving or returning."

"Good. Keep pressure on Sheila, too." Hayes' words were clipped, efficient. "Maybe she slips, gives us more than wig fibers and dead ends."

Silence stretched between them, thick with contemplation. Then, from the doorway, Dr. Laura Evans spoke, her voice cutting through the tension like a scalpel. "Forensic analysis."

Heads turned in unison toward her. She stood framed by the doorway, the epitome of professional calm against the backdrop of frenzied brainstorming. "We've got the hair, the fibers. What if there's more we're not seeing?"

"Like what?" Lee asked, interest piqued.

"Trace elements," Dr. Evans replied, stepping into the room. "Microscopic. Something that ties Sheila directly to the crime scene, or to Marlene."

"Can you do it?" Hayes' question was pointed, urgent.

"Absolutely." Dr. Evans' blue eyes met his, unwavering. "Given the chance, I'll find it. No stone left unturned."

"Then it's settled." Hayes slapped his palm against the table, a sharp report that set their plan into motion. "We go deeper. Forensics leads. Laura, you spearhead this."

"Consider it done." Dr. Evans' confirmation was crisp, her determination reflecting the team's collective resolve.

"Marlene deserves justice," Hayes stated, the name anchoring them all to the heart of their mission.

They rose, a united front against the shadows of doubt. The hunt continued, each member driven by the unspoken vow to unearth the truth, for Marlene, for justice—for closure.

Nodding in consensus, the team fixed their gaze on Dr. Laura Evans. She was already on her feet, a silent promise etched into every line of her stoic face. There would be no half-measures, not with Marlene's justice hanging in the balance.

"Let's get to work," Dr. Evans said, her tone leaving no room for doubt. The investigative rhythm pulsed through the room, syncing with the beat of urgency that thrummed in each of them. They knew the path forward; it was narrower but clearer now, thanks to her.

In the sterile embrace of the crime lab, Dr. Evans donned her white coat like armor. Each snap of her latex gloves marked her readiness for the battle ahead. The evidence lay before her, an array of possibilities shrouded in scientific obscurity. She would unveil its secrets.

She began with the orange wig fibers, tweezing them from their plastic abode with practiced precision. Each fiber found its new home in a labeled vial, sealed against contamination. Next were Sheila's hairs, each a potential link in the chain of guilt. Dr. Evans handled them with equal care, her movements deliberate and meticulous.

"Chain of custody intact," she muttered to herself, logging every detail in the ledger of truth. Protocols were her scripture, and she followed them religiously, ensuring no question could taint the integrity of her findings.

"Sample preservation: check. Cross-contamination: none." Her checklist was methodical, each step a footprint leading deeper into the heart of forensic discovery. Dr. Evans moved with the swift assurance of experience, her mind racing through the possibilities even as her hands performed the dance of due diligence.

Around her, machines whirred, lights blinked, but she was an island of calm in the sea of activity. Nothing existed outside the scope of her analysis—the chance to reveal the hidden narrative woven into the very fibers she now entrusted to science.

"Ready for testing," she announced to the empty room, her voice steady. Yet within those three words thrummed the weight of expectation, the hope of justice, the spark of breakthrough that might just burn away the shadows of uncertainty clinging to Sheila's guilt.

The samples were secure, the investigation reinvigorated. Now, all they needed was for science to speak the language of truth loud enough for the scales of justice to hear.

Dr. Laura Evans' fingers flew over the keyboard, her eyes scanning the list of contacts on her computer screen with practiced ease. She was searching for the best in their fields: textile analysts, DNA specialists, and trace evidence experts. Each email sent and each call made was a step towards unraveling the tangled web of the case at hand.

"Forensic entomologist, check," she murmured, locking in an expert known for deciphering timelines from insect activity. The clock ticked in the background, a reminder that time was both ally and adversary.

"Next, fiber analysis." Her voice was a whisper, as if speaking too loudly might disturb the delicate balance of the investigation.

Days melded into nights, blurring the lines between shifts and breaks. Dr. Evans updated Detective Hayes and Officer Lee with the tenacity of a metronome, each beat a testament to progress.

"DNA sequencing initiated," she reported during one of their briefings, her tone clipped and efficient.

"Any preliminary findings?" Hayes asked, his voice echoing the gravity of their task.

"Too soon. But we're narrowing down the variables," she replied, her blue eyes reflecting both the fatigue and the fierce determination that drove her.

Officer Lee took notes, her pen scratching against paper in a steady cadence. "What about the fibers?"

"Quantitative analysis underway. We'll have a better picture soon," Evans assured them, her confidence not wavering despite the pressure.

Weeks passed. Hayes and Lee digested every update, their anticipation building with each incremental advance. They knew the value of patience in a game where details could make or break a case.

"Cross-referencing databases for the wig fibers now," Dr. Evans announced during a conference call, her voice betraying no hint of the strain that the painstaking process demanded of her.

"Keep us posted, Laura," Hayes responded, his voice a mixture of respect and urgency.

"Always do," she said before ending the call, turning back to the labyrinthine task of piecing together microscopic truths.

In the lab, Dr. Evans was a sentinel, unwavering in her watch over the evidence that spoke in whispers. She liaised with the forensic experts, pieced together their findings like a master weaver crafting a tapestry of facts. The narrative was emerging, thread by thread, and with it, the promise of justice for Marlene.

The clock on the wall ticked monotonously, each second a hammer on the anvils of their patience. Dr. Laura Evans stood before the crime lab's sterile benches, her gaze locked on the sealed evidence bags arrayed like silent sentinels before her. Her hands, clad in latex, hovered above them—a conductor awaiting the symphony's start.

"Any moment now," she muttered to herself, the words barely more than a breath.

Detective Brian Hayes leaned against the cold metal doorway, arms folded across his chest, his eyes the epitome of vigilance. Beside him, Officer Jessica Lee mirrored his stance, her own eyes sharp, surveying the scene with an intensity that had become her trademark.

"Could be it," Hayes said, the hint of anticipation roughening his voice. He checked his watch, impatience etched into the furrow of his brow.

Lee nodded, her hand instinctively reaching up to tug at her collar, a gesture born of restless energy. "The break we need."

Dr. Evans' phone chirped. A message flashed across the screen, stark and demanding attention. She read the text, her lips pressing into a thin line. The forensic experts were ready; the results were in. This was the culmination of countless hours, the apex of meticulous labor.

"Let's go," she announced, her tone crisp, slicing through the tension.

They moved as one, a unit bound by shared resolve. In the lab's hushed confines, the air seemed to hum with the weight of potential revelations. Each step they took resonated with purpose, every heartbeat a drumroll to destiny's door.

"Results could tie Sheila directly to the crime scene," Evans stated, the facts laid bare, unadorned yet laden with implication.

"Or give us nothing." Hayes' voice was gruff, a reminder of the stakes at play.

"Either way, we find out now," Lee added, her optimism undiminished.

The forensic team awaited them, guardians of truth in white coats. Dr. Evans took the lead, her hand steady as she accepted the printout from the lead analyst. The data was a hieroglyph, a code that only she could decipher in this crucial moment.

She scanned the page, her eyes tracing lines, numbers, graphs. And then, the corners of her mouth twitched—an almost imperceptible movement, but enough. Enough for hope to flare in Hayes' and Lee's chests.

"We've got something," Dr. Evans said, allowing herself the hint of a smile.

Hayes stepped closer, his experience telling him not to celebrate too soon, yet unable to quell the rising tide of expectancy. Lee's pen was poised over her notebook, ready to record what might be the turning point in their investigation.

"Details," Hayes demanded, his voice a low growl of controlled zeal.

"Give me a few hours to confirm," Evans replied, her professionalism a dam against premature excitement.

"Then we'll know if we can charge Sheila for Marlene's murder," Lee finished for her, the sentence hanging between them—a promise, a possibility, a plea.

Chapter 9

Detective Brian Hayes leaned in closer, his blue eyes scanning the labyrinth of red strings that crisscrossed the evidence board. Photographs of Marlene, smiling, unaware of her fate, seemed to mock their lack of progress. Officer Jessica Lee stood beside him, her brown eyes fixated on the cluster of notes and timelines.

"Dead ends," Brian grumbled, tapping a finger against an image of Sheila. "Circumstantial at best."

Jessica nodded, frustration etching her features. "Not enough to charge her. We need a break in this case."

The room was silent, save for the ticking clock—a reminder of time slipping away. Then, Jessica's phone shattered the quiet. She snatched it up, her posture rigid with anticipation.

"Lee here."

Brian watched her face intently, reading the subtle shift in her expression as she listened. He knew that look—potential lead. She scribbled furiously on a pad.

"Understood. Thanks for coming forward." Her voice was a low whisper now, but Brian could hear the urgency bleeding through.

She hung up, turning to Brian, her eyes alight. "Got a tip," she said, her tone clipped with excitement. "Anonymous. Claims they know where Sheila hid evidence."

"Where?" Brian asked, already reaching for his notepad.

"An old storage unit, off the highway. The caller was certain."

"Let's move," Brian said, pushing back from the table. They had no time to waste. Every second counted now. Every clue was a step closer to justice for Marlene.

The moment Jessica ended the call, a surge of adrenaline coursed through her. She sprang from her chair, eyes locked with Brian's. "Storage unit," she blurted out, snatching her jacket from the back of her seat. "We have to check it out."

"Let's roll," Brian responded, his voice taut with anticipation. He stood up, the chair screeching against the floor, grabbed his coat, and strode towards the door, his every step exuding a seasoned urgency.

Jessica was right behind him, her mind racing with the possibilities of what they might find. They dashed through the precinct, navigating the maze of desks and uniformed bodies with practiced ease. Colleagues glanced up, sensing the sudden burst of energy, but the two officers were already past, their focus narrowed to the task at hand.

Outside, the cool air slapped their faces as they hurried to the unmarked car. Jessica took the driver's seat, her hands gripping the wheel firmly. The engine roared to life, and they peeled out of the parking lot, sirens silent but hearts pounding loud in their ears.

The city blurred by as they made their way to the outskirts, where the buildings grew sparse and the bright veneer of downtown faded. The address led them to a dilapidated apartment complex, a relic of better times now succumbing to decay.

Pulling up to the curb, they surveyed the structure. Its windows were like vacant eyes, staring out into nothingness. Jessica's pulse quickened as she stepped out of the car, noting how the building loomed ominously against the overcast sky.

They entered the hallway, dimly lit by flickering fluorescent lights that cast eerie shadows on the walls. Paint peeled like old scars, revealing layers of neglect beneath. A faint smell of stale cigarettes pervaded the air, mingling with the musty scent of abandonment.

"Watch your step," Brian murmured, his eyes scanning the corridor for any sign of danger—or opportunity. His detective's instincts honed over decades, he moved with a quiet confidence that belied the tension coiling within him.

Jessica nodded, her senses heightened as they progressed down the hall. Each creaking floorboard felt like a whisper of secrets long buried, each numbered door a potential vault of evidence that could break the case wide open.

They were close now, Jessica thought, closer than ever to finding the truth. And whatever lay hidden within these walls would bring them one step nearer to justice for Marlene.

Brian raised a fist, three solid knocks reverberating through the apartment's flimsy door. "Police," he announced, his voice firm, the badge in his other hand catching what little light there was. Beside him, Jessica stood poised, her gaze fixed on the peephole, as if willing the occupant to hurry.

Seconds stretched into a tense eternity before the sound of shuffling feet approached from the other side. A shadow flickered across the peephole, and then the door cracked open just wide enough to reveal a sliver of a man's face—haggard, eyes clouded with confusion.

"Can we help you?" The voice was wary, the question more of a defense than an offer.

"Detective Brian Hayes, and this is Officer Jessica Lee," Brian introduced methodically, displaying his credentials. Jessica mirrored the action, her expression all business. "We need to search your apartment."

The man's eyes darted from Brian to Jessica, then back again, as if searching for an escape in their steady gaze. His hand gripped the door, knuckles whitening—a silent battle waged behind those bloodshot eyes.

"Search? What for?"

"Potential evidence related to an ongoing investigation," Jessica chimed in, her tone leaving no room for argument. "It's imperative we look around."

A long moment passed—the man seemed to weigh his options, the residue of fear clinging to the edges of his hesitation. Then, with a sigh that spoke of resignation, or perhaps something darker, he swung the door open wider.

"Fine," he muttered, stepping back into the chaos of his living space. "But I haven't done anything wrong."

"Thank you," Brian said, crossing the threshold with Jessica close behind. The air inside was stale, heavy with the scent of old takeout and lost time. They were in now, and every instinct told them they were on the right path. The hunt for truth beckoned from within the disarray.

The living room was a graveyard of past meals and forgotten news. Detective Brian Hayes navigated around towers of newspapers, his blue eyes scanning for anything out of the ordinary. Officer Jessica Lee followed suit, her hands gloved, ready to sift through the detritus of a life in disarray. They moved with purpose, each corner of the room whispering potential clues.

"Check behind the furniture," Brian directed, his voice low but firm. Jessica nodded, pushing against a sagging couch to reveal nothing but dust bunnies and a few loose coins.

"Nothing here," she confirmed, disappointment lacing her words.

Brian grunted, his attention caught by a bulky armchair. He shoved it aside. More nothing. Frustration knotted his brow. Marlene deserved justice. They needed to find it here.

"Keep looking," he urged, the keen edge of his determination cutting through the gloom.

Jessica's ponytail swayed as she continued her systematic search, lifting cushions and opening drawers. Time was slipping away like sand through their fingers.

Then, in the closet, amid a clutter of clothing and forgotten junk, Brian's hand brushed against the back panel. A hollow sound. His heart rate spiked—an anomaly. He pressed, leaned, shifted until—a click.

"Jess," he called softly, the single word heavy with implication.

She was at his side in an instant, watching as he eased the false back open. Inside, a box. Dust motes danced in the beam of light from Brian's flashlight as he lifted the lid with reverence.

"Photographs... documents," he muttered, thumbing through the contents. Each piece could be the key they were searching for, the break in the wall that had kept Sheila shielded from consequence.

"Could this be it?" Jessica breathed, her voice tinged with cautious hope.

"Maybe," Brian replied, his pulse thrumming in his temples. "Let's find out."

Together, they plunged into the past, laid bare in faded ink and captured moments. The truth was close, Brian could feel it. It had to be here.

Brian's fingers sifted through the detritus of someone else's life, old receipts, postcards from places long forgotten. But among them, something stood out—a photograph. It was worn at the edges, the colors faded to a soft patina of age.

"Jess, look." Brian's voice was steady but insistent.

She leaned over his shoulder, her breath quickening as she caught sight of the image: Sheila and Mike, arms draped around each other, grinning before an old carnival backdrop. The timestamp in the corner was a whisper from the past, a date that lined up too neatly with the timeline of Marlene's disappearance.

"God," Jessica murmured, her eyes narrowing. "That's just days before..."

"Exactly." Brian's reply was terse. The photo was circumstantial at best, but it was a connection—one they couldn't ignore.

Jessica's gaze shifted, flickering across the room, every surface a potential clue. Then, a glint caught her eye—metal reflecting the dim light. She stepped toward it, pushing aside a pile of discarded clothes. A safe, small and squat, sat wedged in the corner, its presence incongruous amidst the squalor.

"Brian!" Her voice was a whip-crack of excitement.

He joined her, following her pointed finger to the safe. Locked. Of course, it was locked. Jessica's jaw set, her eyes alight with the fire of challenge. This could be it—the tangible link to Sheila they needed.

"Can we get it open?" Brian asked.

Jessica nodded, the determination in her eyes mirrored by the firm set of her lips. That safe wasn't just a box of steel—it was a barrier to justice, and she would tear it down.

Jessica crouched, her breaths shallow. The safe's dial taunted her, cold and unyielding. She touched it; the metal was icy against her fingertips. Sweat beaded on her forehead, hands trembling with each tiny click.

"Come on," she whispered, as if coaxing a secret from a stubborn child.

Numbers spun, a combination guessed from years of experience and gut instinct. Click. Click. Click. Time hung suspended, every second a drumbeat in her ears. Brian watched over her shoulder, his silence a heavy weight.

"Almost..." Her voice trailed off, focus narrowing to the feel of the dial under her skin. Another number, another hope.

The mechanism inside the safe gave a faint, mocking laugh—a refusal. Jessica's heart hammered, but her resolve hardened. Adjust. Twist. Nudge. She tried again, refusing defeat.

"Anytime now," Brian muttered, impatience threading his tone. He checked over his shoulder, the ever-present threat of being discovered looming like a shadow.

"Shh," Jessica hissed. This was a dance of digits and wills, one she was determined to lead.

Click. A different sound. Softer. Deeper. The tumblers fell into place with a satisfying thud that whispered of victory. Jessica's breath caught. She turned the handle. The door swung open.

"Got it!" The urgency in her voice matched the racing of her pulse.

Inside, the safe revealed its secrets: a stack of documents, their edges crisp and untouched by time, and a single flash drive, black and innocuous, yet screaming importance.

"Jesus, Jess," Brian breathed out. His eyes were wide, reflecting the gravity of their find.

Jessica reached in, her fingers brushing the papers. Each sheet could be the downfall of a killer, the end of a chase. She plucked the flash drive from its resting place, its weight nothing and everything all at once.

"Look at this..." Her words trailed off into awe, her mind already racing with the possibilities.

Their eyes met, and in that silent exchange, they understood the magnitude of what lay before them. They had uncovered something vital, a turning point in the case that could tip the scales of justice.

"Let's see what we've got," said Brian, but as their anticipation peaked, the chapter ended, leaving a question hanging in the air, palpable and unresolved. What truths did these silent witnesses hold?

Chapter 10

Mike Thompson perched on the edge of his seat, a coiled spring in a courtroom packed with anticipation. His tailored suit felt like armor, albeit ineffective against the looming verdict. The sharp click of the judge's gavel punctured the silence, reverberating off the walls and through Mike's core.

"Will the defendant please rise."

The command was routine, the situation anything but. A collective breath held, the air thick with tension. Mike stood, his posture erect, betraying none of the turmoil churning inside. He faced the judge, the epitome of confidence eroding under the weight of judicial scrutiny.

"Mr. Thompson," the judge began, voice echoing, "this court finds you guilty as charged." Each word landed like a hammer to Mike's future, stripping away layers of charm and bravado.

Around him, the room seemed to sway. Whispers fluttered like moths to a flame — each syllable a confirmation of his fate. Faces blurred into a sea of judgment, an audience to his downfall.

Guilty. The word hung in the air, a specter over Mike's well-crafted persona. His heart raced, the conviction a tangible force pressing down on him. Eyes wide, he stood motionless, the reality of prison bars closing in.

Mike's world, once ruled by deals and deception, shrank to this single moment of truth. And the truth was merciless.

The gavel's echo faded, leaving behind an oppressive stillness. Mike's gaze darted frantically across the courtroom, a silent plea for an ally. His once assured demeanor crumbled; in its wake, raw panic surfaced. He sought Sheila, desperate for one steadfast gaze in a sea of schadenfreude.

Sheila reclined, detached from the chaos she had orchestrated with such precision. Her red hair, a fiery contrast to the courtroom's drab palette, spilled over the back of her seat. The corners of her mouth curled into a smug smile as she observed the man who believed he could outsmart her.

Mike's search ended at the back of the room, but not with the solidarity he yearned for. Instead, he found the architect of his ruin, basking in the glow of victory. Her green eyes sparkled, not with tears of compassion, but with the cold glint of triumph.

Their eyes met across the chasm of the courtroom, a silent war waged in a single glance. Mike's shock morphed into seething anger as he absorbed the betrayal etched into Sheila's smirking features. Accusations flew silently between them, unspoken yet deafening. His glare was a dagger; hers, a shield gleaming with victory. She didn't flinch.

Years peeled away like old paint, revealing a changed man stepping through the prison gates. Freedom's first breath was bitter, laden with lost time and tarnished dreams. Mike's eyes, once sharp with cunning, now scanned the crowd with weary bitterness. A lifetime ago, he would've expected limousines, flashing cameras. Today, there was only the heavy weight of reality pressing against his chest.

He searched for Sheila, despite everything. Her presence was a torment he couldn't escape, an addiction formed from shared sin and ambition. But the sea of faces brought no sign of fiery red hair or piercing green eyes. No trace of the woman who'd once promised the world and delivered ruin.

Relief mingled with resentment; he was free but forever marked. There was no victory lap, no cheers. Just the unforgiving pavement under his shoes and the vast, uncertain horizon stretching out before him. Mike Thompson was out, but at what cost?

Mike's gaze cut through the throng, a blade searching for one target. And there she was. Sheila leaned against the prison's outer wall, a concrete queen on her cold throne. Red hair ablumed in the sunlight, green eyes glinted with something dark and triumphant. Her lips curved, not quite a smile, but a signal of victory. She was waiting, as if she had never doubted this day would come.

Mike's first step toward freedom faltered. His heart, caged for years, now beat against its prison of flesh and bone. He strode across the no man's land separating past from future, his every step heavy with the gravity of their shared history.

Their eyes met, a silent clash echoing the courtroom's silent war. Mike halted inches from Sheila, his presence demanding an audience. The distance closed, their bodies pressed into a hollow embrace. It was the hug of survivors clinging to the wreckage of their lives, where warmth once blossomed, now only the chill of betrayal remained.

"Mike," Sheila murmured into his ear, her voice a siren's whisper, masking the jagged edges of their reality.

"Sheila," he replied, the name tasting like poison on his tongue. They parted, just enough to survey the damage written in the lines of each other's faces. A cruel reminder of time stolen and innocence pawned for ambition's sake.

Together, they stood at the precipice of what came next, their embrace a fragile truce in a world that had turned its back on them both.

Mike's gaze followed the gray, nondescript sedan as it crawled to a stop by the curb. The vehicle—a far cry from the glossy machines he once paraded at the lot—was their ride, their chariot into an uncertain future. They slid into the back seat, the door thudding shut with finality.

"Where to?" The driver's voice was indifferent, a mere backdrop to the tension that crackled between Mike and Sheila.

"Doesn't matter," Sheila said, her eyes never leaving Mike. "Just drive."

The car pulled away, leaving behind the cold steel of prison bars and the echo of clanging gates. Inside, silence reigned until Mike shattered it with a bitter laugh.

"Look at us," he spat, his words sharp as the suits he used to wear. "You happy now?"

Sheila turned towards him, her green eyes burning with defiance. "This was your plan, Mike. I just... played along."

"Played along?" His voice rose, incredulous. "You were there, every step. Pushing, scheming."

"Because you needed me to! Without me, you'd have been nothing but a small-time crook!"

Mike's face tightened, the muscles working as he processed her words. The realization hit him like a punch to the gut. Sheila, with her red hair like flames, had ignited their descent into crime. It was her lack of empathy, her manipulative nature that had fanned the sparks of his own dark impulses into a raging inferno.

"Nothing?" He leaned closer, his voice a low growl. "I built that business. You just twisted it for your own gain."

"Twisted?" Sheila's laugh was cold, devoid of humor. "We wanted the same things, Mike. Money. Power. Don't pretend you're above it all."

He recoiled from her, staring out the window at the blur of the world passing by. The memories came in flashes—late nights, whispered plans, the thrill of the con. But beneath it all, there was Sheila, always Sheila, pulling the strings, orchestrating their downfall.

"Is that what you think?" Mike's reflection stared back at him from the glass, a man he barely recognized. "That I'm just like you?"

Sheila reached out, her fingers grazing his arm. "We're survivors, Mike. We can still—"

"Survivors?" He shook off her touch, anger bubbling to the surface. "No. You survived. You thrived. You used me."

The quiet that followed was loaded, a ticking bomb between them. Sheila's smile had vanished, replaced by a look that was calculating, even predatory. She knew she had him, even now.

"Whatever helps you sleep at night, darling," she said softly.

Mike turned away, his mind racing. Every second with her was a step further into darkness. A partnership borne of greed had become a cage, and he knew one thing with chilling clarity: Sheila Chambers had been his ruin, and now she could be his vengeance.

Mike stood rigid, the free air hitting him like a shock of cold water. Sheila was there, just beyond the gate, waiting for him—a lone figure that seemed to hold all the cards. Her stance was relaxed, but her eyes were anything but; they gleamed with the sharpness of someone always playing an angle.

"Freedom suits you," she said as he approached, her voice smooth, betraying none of the bitterness from their last encounter.

"Does it?" Mike replied, his tone flat. He was out, yes, but the taste of liberty was sour, tainted by the schemes that had landed him behind bars in the first place.

Sheila stepped closer, her scent overwhelming—like a potent mix designed to cloud judgment. "We're not done, Mike. This is just a setback."

"Setback?" His eyebrow lifted skeptically. The word felt inadequate for the years lost, the reputation shredded.

"Think about it," Sheila pressed on, her voice dropping to a conspiratorial whisper. "People love a good comeback story. We can spin this. We still have contacts, resources..."

He wanted to scoff at her audacity, yet part of him clung to the allure of the con, the game. Sheila knew that part of him well—too well.

"Start over?" Mike asked, the idea dangling before him like bait.

"Exactly." Sheila's smile returned, a predator baring teeth. "Together, we're unstoppable. You know that."

His resolve wavered under her gaze, the familiar pull of ambition winding its way through his thoughts. She was offering redemption wrapped in the same cloth as their past sins.

"Mike," she said, softer now, taking his hand. "We're stronger as one. Let's show them what we're made of."

And there it was—the hook. Despite everything, the prospect tugged at him. Sheila's grip was firm, her touch a tether drawing him back into a world he should've known to leave behind.

They stepped forward, their steps syncing as they moved away from the prison gates. Hand in hand, their shadows merged on the pavement—a dark dance of two silhouettes bound by more than just vows. Their marriage was a partnership sealed not by love, but by the shared hunger for power and the relentless drive to bend the world to their will.

As the gate clanged shut behind them, Mike felt the weight of the metal echo within him—a reminder of what had been and what could be again. But this time, he would be ready for Sheila's games. He had to be.

Daniel leaned against the hood of his car, parked on a rise that overlooked the prison gates. Binoculars pressed to his eyes, he tracked every movement below. His jaw was set, muscles tensing as the two familiar figures emerged into the waning daylight.

They were holding hands. A show for the world, perhaps, or a genuine link between co-conspirators; it didn't matter. They looked free. Too free for what they'd done.

Anger simmered within him, a tight ball of heat in his chest. His grip on the binoculars tightened until his knuckles whitened. They shouldn't be allowed to just walk out, not after everything.

His mother's face flashed in his mind—her smile, once so warm, now a memory tinged with loss and betrayal. Marlene deserved better. She deserved justice.

The couple paused, heads close together, whispering conspiracies Daniel could only guess at. His heart thudded, a drumbeat urging action.

Sheila laughed, the sound carrying faintly up the hill. It was carefree, mocking the gravity of their crimes. Mike's hand squeezed hers in response, complicit even in silence.

"Never again," Daniel whispered to himself. The words were a vow etched sharp and deep.

He lowered the binoculars, his gaze hardening as the couple faded into the distance. Sadness tugged at him, a ghostly hand on his shoulder. But stronger still was the resolve that anchored his feet to the ground.

He would dig. He would follow. Every dirty secret, every lie they thought buried—he would bring into the light.

Marlene's honor demanded no less.

Chapter 11

The precinct buzzed with a different kind of energy that morning, a palpable charge that hadn't been felt in years. It was the sound of old ghosts being stirred from their rest, the whispers of a cold case thawing under the scrutiny of fresh eyes.

Detective Sarah Collins paced the narrow confines of her newly assigned office, her gaze fixed on the worn file that lay open on her desk. Marlene Thompson's smiling face looked up at her from a photograph clipped to the folder, the image frozen in time, oblivious to the decade and a half that had slipped by since her light was extinguished.

Beside her, Forensic Analyst Mark Thompson (no relation to Marlene) was already poring over the contents of the box labeled "Thompson, Marlene - 2008" with an intensity that matched her own. His fingers sifted through evidence bags with reverence, as if touching sacred relics. They were a team built on the cornerstone of unsolved mysteries; their reputation for unraveling the forgotten threads of justice preceded them.

"Collins, any luck?" Mark asked, head still buried in the pile of reports.

"Still looking," Sarah responded curtly, her focus unwavering. She had a knack for spotting the out-of-place detail, the overlooked clue, the break in the pattern. And she knew that somewhere within the confines of those tattered pages lay the key to unlocking the truth.

Fifteen years had passed since the day Marlene Thompson's lifeless body was found in her suburban home, a tragedy that had sent ripples through the community and left a family shattered. Her husband Mike, once a charismatic businessman, now carried a shadow behind his confident stride. The whispers of his dealings hovered around him like a persistent fog.

And then there was Daniel, the son who grew up in the long shadow of unanswered questions, his youth stolen by the need to fill the hollow void left by his mother's absence. His resolve to seek answers had only hardened with time, his eyes now reflecting a pain that went far beyond his years.

The original investigators had retired with the burden of the unsolved case weighing heavily on their conscience, while the public's memory of Marlene never quite faded. Her case was the ghost story parents whispered about, the cautionary tale that kept the neighborhood watch ever vigilant.

"Thompson, we need to find what they missed," Sarah stated, her tone imbued with a sense of urgency that mirrored the task ahead.

"Agreed," Mark replied, his eyes never leaving the evidence. "We'll get justice for her, Collins. No stone unturned."

Sarah turned back to the file, her mind sifting through the details like a miner panning for gold. Every witness statement, every piece of evidence, every lead that went cold over the years—it was all part of a larger puzzle that she was determined to solve.

Because for Detective Sarah Collins and Forensic Analyst Mark Thompson, this wasn't just another case. It was a promise to a family torn apart by tragedy, a vow to a community haunted by uncertainty, and a commitment to the memory of a woman whose gentle smile had been snuffed out too soon.

And they wouldn't rest until the truth was laid bare, until Marlene Thompson could finally rest in peace.

Sarah Collins fanned out the crime scene photos across her desk, a mosaic of tragedy laid bare under the harsh fluorescent lights. She leaned in, her gaze sharp as she scrutinized each image, searching for the smallest detail that might have been overlooked. Mark Thompson hovered nearby, his fingers stained with ink as he pored over the forensic reports, his brows knitted in concentration.

"Look at this," Sarah's voice cut through the silence, more statement than question. "The position of the lamp—it's inconsistent with the witness accounts."

Mark abandoned his report, joining Sarah to study the photo in question. "You're right. It was supposedly knocked over during the struggle, but here it's upright, on the other side of the room."

"Could be sloppy police work," Sarah mused, "or something more deliberate." Her words were like flint, sparking the possibility of new leads from cold ashes.

They moved methodically, dissecting every witness statement with clinical precision, cross-referencing times and alibis. Discrepancies surfaced like air bubbles, subtle but significant. A neighbor who claimed to have heard nothing, yet the coroner's timeline suggested otherwise. A delivery man whose statement was never fully corroborated.

"Collins, check this out," Mark said, tapping a line in a faded report. "Forensics never followed up on the partial shoe print in the mud outside the window. Standard issue back then, but now..."

"Now we can do better," Sarah finished for him, her pulse quickening with the scent of a trail gone cold but not dead.

Their determination was a palpable force in the cramped office, an unspoken pact between them to dredge up the truth. They sifted through evidence, looking for connections, patterns, anything that might lead to the break they desperately needed.

"Everyone assumed the husband, Mike, was just a charming businessman," Sarah pondered aloud, thumbing through Mike Thompson's file. "But charm can be a convenient mask."

"Or maybe it was someone else entirely," Mark countered, his analytical mind considering every angle. "Someone who knew her routine, who could blend into the background."

"Either way, we're missing something," Sarah admitted, frustration edging her words. "And I'm not letting this go until I find it."

Hours turned into days, days into weeks, each passing moment fueling their resolve. The task force pushed forward, relentless, the specter of Marlene Thompson urging them from beyond the grave, her case a puzzle begging to be solved.

"Sarah, if we look at the sequence of events leading up to that night..." Mark started, trailing off as a new theory began to form.

"Then maybe we can start to piece together her last hours," Sarah finished, a spark igniting in her eyes. They were close; she could feel it in her bones.

Together, they dove back into the abyss of the past, determined to bring light to the darkness that had swallowed Marlene's story. There was justice to be served, and they would settle for nothing less.

The fluorescent glow of the lab cast stark shadows across Sarah Collins' face as she watched Dr. Laura Evans guide a swab across the slide. Fifteen years had done nothing to degrade Marlene's last whispers etched in blood - whispers that advanced DNA testing might finally amplify into a scream for justice.

"New markers," Dr. Evans stated, her voice a metronome of precision. "We'll run them against the latest databases."

"Any partials we overlooked?" Sarah asked, her gaze locked on the meticulous movements of the forensic expert.

"Enhanced fingerprint analysis is next," Dr. Evans replied without looking up. "The tech's leagues ahead of what we had back then."

Sarah nodded, the energy of potential breakthroughs crackling in the sterile air. Mark Thompson leaned over a monitor nearby, his fingers dancing across the keyboard, summoning high-definition images of prints left untouched by time but not by technology.

"Got something," Mark announced abruptly, zooming in on a ridge detail previously indiscernible. Sarah's heart thumped a rapid beat - each new revelation a step closer to the truth.

"Let's loop in Dr. Rodriguez," Sarah suggested, adrenaline sharpening her focus. "We need her read on this."

On cue, the screen split, and Dr. Emily Rodriguez's composed features filled half the frame. A forensic psychologist whose insights cut through facades like scalpels, Emily was their bridge to the minds behind the evidence.

"Notice the hesitancy here?" Emily's cursor hovered over a section of the print. "Could indicate reluctance. Or fear."

"Or an outsider not entirely comfortable at the crime scene," Mark chimed in, his brain already sifting through the implications.

"Exactly," Emily affirmed. "Let's consider scenarios where our suspect might have felt compelled to proceed despite reservations."

"Compulsion, hesitation, fear," Sarah mused. "That's a psychological cocktail that could narrow our search."

"Keep me updated on the DNA results," Dr. Evans interjected, her blue eyes never leaving the scope. "Every second counts now."

"Will do," Sarah promised, feeling the weight of years lifting with the promise of science and psychology lighting their path forward. They were racing against time, but the pace invigorated them. Justice was patient, but they were not.

The interrogation room was stark, the air stale with tension. Detective Sarah Collins sat across from a man who claimed to remember nothing new about the night Marlene Thompson died. Beside her, Mark Thompson tapped his pen in rapid succession, a metronome to Sarah's growing impatience.

"Think," Sarah urged, her voice a blend of command and entreaty. "Anything you saw could be vital."

The man shook his head, his eyes averted. "It's been so long, Detective. I've told you everything."

Mark exchanged a glance with Sarah, his expression tight with frustration. They moved through witness after witness, the hours stretching thin, each interview folding into the next like a relentless wave of déjà vu.

"Dead end," Mark muttered as they exited another fruitless meeting.

"Next," Sarah replied, terse. Her resolve was steel; surrender was not in her vocabulary.

They approached Daniel Thompson, Marlene's son, whose youthful face was etched with the hardships of loss. His hands clenched unsteadily as he recounted the events surrounding his mother's death for the countless time.

"Anything out of place that day, any detail," Mark prodded, watching Daniel's every micro-expression.

"Nothing. It was just a normal day until... until it wasn't," Daniel replied, his voice strained.

"Thank you, Daniel. We'll find the person responsible," Sarah promised, though the assurance rang hollow even to her own ears.

Back at their desks, surrounded by stacks of files and crime scene photos, the weight of unanswered questions pressed down on them.

"Let's go over it again," Mark said, determination hardening his features. He pulled up a map of the neighborhood, dotted with markers and notes.

"Everything we need is right here. We're just not seeing it," Sarah responded, her gaze fierce as she leaned over the evidence spread between them.

"Back to square one," Mark sighed, but his eyes were alive, searching, unyielding.

"Square one is where we start, not where we finish," Sarah countered, her mind racing through possibilities, angles, leads.

They worked in sync, fueled by the need for answers, chasing down every thread, every inconsistency. Each dead end steeled them further, each false lead sharpened their focus. The truth was elusive, a specter in the fog, but Sarah Collins and Mark Thompson were relentless hunters.

"Something's got to give," Sarah whispered, more to herself than to Mark. And when it did, they would be ready.

Sarah shuffled through the array of crime scene photographs strewn across her desk. Mark sat opposite, his eyes flitting between witness statements and forensic reports. The room was silent save for the occasional rustle of paper and the soft clicking of a computer mouse. Fifteen years had not dimmed the urgency in their actions; if anything, it fueled them.

"Wait," Mark's voice cut through the silence, tentative yet laced with a potential promise. "This photo... Has anyone followed up on the background? There, beyond the alley."

Sarah leaned over, her eyes narrowing as she scrutinized the image. A figure, barely discernible, was captured in the periphery—a specter from the past that nobody seemed to have noticed. It wasn't much, but in cold cases, 'not much' could mean everything.

"Get a magnification on this, enhance it," she ordered, her detective instincts seizing upon the thread of possibility. She sensed the subtle shift in the room's atmosphere, like the quiet tension before a storm.

"Enhancing now," Mark replied, his fingers already dancing across the keyboard. The grainy figure slowly became clearer, inching them toward a revelation that had eluded everyone for so long.

As the printer hummed, spitting out the enhanced image, Sarah paced the floor, her mind racing. Each step was a silent drumbeat, each breath a call to arms. This could be the break they desperately needed, the clue that would lead them out of the labyrinth of dead ends and into the light of truth.

"Got something else," Mark said, his tone steady but his hand betraying a slight tremor as he held out another document—an overlooked witness statement that contradicted earlier testimony.

"Good catch," Sarah acknowledged, snatching the paper. Her eyes devoured the text, absorbing every word, every nuance. Discrepancies jumped out at her, forming patterns in the chaos. There was no time for celebration, only work—the relentless pursuit that had become their signature.

"Mark, cross-reference this with the timeline we have. I want to know where everyone was when this statement was made," she commanded, already reaching for her phone to set up interviews.

They dove back into the depths, the puzzle of Marlene's murder sprawling before them, demanding to be solved. Every piece was a life, a memory, a secret. They were the seekers of hidden truths, the bearers of justice for Marlene and her family.

"Whatever it takes," Mark muttered, almost to himself, as he lined up timelines and witness accounts into the early hours. Fatigue clawed at their resolve, but it was no match for their determination.

"Whatever it takes," Sarah echoed, her eyes never leaving the evidence.

Sarah's gaze fixed on the faded photograph, the edges worn from time and fingerprints. Mark stood silent beside her, his eyes tracing invisible lines across the crime scene sprawled out on the table. Their minds synchronized in their search for the elusive truth that had slipped through the cracks fifteen years ago.

"Wait," Mark breathed, his finger hovering over a segment of the photograph—a partial print near the edge of Marlene's kitchen counter, previously dismissed as irrelevant. His voice held the weight of discovery, a sharp edge cutting through the fog of fatigue.

"Enhance this," Sarah said, urgency lacing her demand. She leaned closer, her pulse quickening, as the image on the screen grew clearer with each passing second.

Pixels danced and realigned, revealing the whorls and ridges of a fingerprint. Not just any fingerprint, but one that didn't belong to Marlene or her family. The room seemed to shrink around them, the air charged with potential.

"Is this..." Mark trailed off, unable to finish the sentence.

"New evidence," Sarah confirmed, her words clipped with excitement. "It's not in the system. It wasn't checked." Her mind raced, piecing together the implications while her hands already dialed the number for the lab.

"Get me Forensics," she said into the phone, her tone brooking no argument.

The silence that followed was pregnant with possibilities. Both of them knew the gravity of what lay before them—a tangible thread to the killer that had evaded them for over a decade.

"Could be our guy," Mark murmured, his eyes locked on the screen, the magnified print a testament to their unwavering determination.

"Could be," Sarah echoed, her heart hammering against her ribs. They were close, closer than anyone had been since the day Marlene's life was stolen away.

The click of an incoming call broke the trance. Forensics was on the line, ready to analyze the print. Sarah relayed the information, her words efficient, devoid of the emotion roiling inside her.

"Run it against everything. Old cases, current databases, watch lists," she instructed, her mind already leaping ahead.

"Will do, Detective Collins. We're on it," came the reply, crisp and professional.

They hung up, and the room fell silent once more. Sarah turned to Mark, her eyes alight with the fire of purpose.

"Let's prepare to move. Once we get a match, we need to be ready."

"Ready to bring him down," Mark agreed, the corners of his mouth lifting in a grim smile.

The chapter closed with a sense of imminent revelation, the air thick with anticipation. The task force stood on the precipice of a breakthrough, the kind that could shatter the stillness of the cold case and echo through the halls of justice. Who did the print belong to? How would this new piece of the puzzle fit into the larger picture?

The answer lay just beyond the horizon, tantalizingly close, promising to shed light on the shadow that had loomed over Marlene's memory for far too long.

Chapter 12

Detective Brian Hayes flipped the manila envelope, its contents decisive and damning. Beside him, Officer Jessica Lee leaned over, her eyes locked on the lab report that lay between them. The DNA match was irrefutable; Sheila's red hair fibers entangled in the fabric of the clown's abandoned getaway car.

"Got her," Brian muttered, a grim satisfaction settling in his gut.

"Finally," Jessica breathed out, her voice a mix of relief and resolve. She straightened up, reaching for her radio.

Brian's hands moved with practiced swiftness, dialing numbers on his phone to summon the team. Time was of the essence, and every second squandered was another moment Sheila could slip through their fingers.

"Team brief, five minutes," he announced into the receiver, his tone clipped and commanding.

Jessica confirmed the location of Sheila's arrest warrant with dispatch, her words crisp and clear. "Warrant confirmed for Sheila Chambers. Immediate execution."

"Copy that, Officer Lee," crackled the response.

The precinct buzzed with sudden energy as officers mobilized, grabbing vests and checking weapons. Brian watched them, his blue eyes piercing through the organized chaos. This was it—the culmination of sleepless nights and dogged pursuit.

"Let's move out," he ordered, leading the charge toward the exit.

Jessica followed close behind, her ponytail swinging with each determined step. Her heart hammered in her chest, adrenaline flooding her system. This was more than an arrest; it was justice clawing its way to the surface.

"Brian," she called out, catching up to him, "we've got this."

He nodded, a tight smile breaking through his usually stern expression. "We do, Officer Lee. Today we make sure of it."

They stepped out into the cool air, the morning sun just beginning to crest the horizon. As they climbed into the unmarked vehicle, the gravity of the moment settled around them. They were about to take down one of the most cunning adversaries they had ever faced. But the evidence was on their side, and so was the law. Today, they would not falter.

Red and blue lights bathed the pre-dawn street in a silent, urgent glow as Detective Brian Hayes surveyed Sheila's modest suburban home. Every window was dark; the calm before the storm. Beside him, Officer Jessica Lee checked her weapon one last time, her movements deliberate, her eyes focused. The air was charged with anticipation, each officer mentally bracing for the task at hand.

"Team ready?" Brian's voice cut through the tension like a knife.

"Ready," came the affirmative murmurs, steely and low.

Brian nodded, his gaze never leaving the house. "Remember, she's smart. Don't underestimate her." He spoke with the conviction of a man who had seen it all — except perhaps not quite like Sheila Chambers.

Jessica's breath formed clouds in the chill, her fingers tingling with a mix of cold and adrenaline. She acknowledged Brian's words with a determined glance. This was the moment they'd been working towards, relentlessly piecing together evidence, chasing down leads. Now, they stood on the precipice of retribution.

"Go!" Brian commanded, his voice barely above a whisper but carrying the weight of authority.

Like a well-oiled machine, the team converged on the house. They moved swiftly, boots barely making a sound on the dew-covered grass. Doors were breached, the silence of the neighborhood shattered by the unmistakable sound of forced entry.

"Police! Hands where we can see them!" Jessica's command echoed through the now-illuminated hallway as they burst into Sheila's sanctuary.

Sheila, caught mid-step in the dimly lit living room, turned, her green eyes wide with shock. The audacious red of her hair seemed to ignite under the sudden onslaught of flashlight beams. For a split second, the world hung still, then chaos resumed its dance.

"Down on the ground! Down on the ground now!" officers shouted, their commands overlapping in the frenzy.

Sheila dropped, her expression unreadable, as officers secured her hands behind her back. Brian stepped forward, his presence commanding the space.

"Shiela Chambers, you are under arrest for the murder of Marlene Hutchinson," he declared, his tone brooking no argument. "You have the right to remain silent. Anything you say can and will be used against you in a court of law."

As he read her rights, the commotion settled into a procedural hum. Officers swept the house, securing evidence, while others escorted Sheila outside. Brian watched, a silent sentinel, as the final piece of this twisted puzzle clicked into place.

Justice, at long last, was in motion.

The handcuffs clicked around her wrists, cold and unyielding. Sheila's pulse hammered in her ears, a stark counterpoint to the surreal calm that descended upon her. Shock rippled through her frame, a momentary lapse in the armor she had meticulously forged over years of scheming and survival.

"Is this a joke?" she spat out, her voice sharp as shattered glass. The room blurred at the edges, reality skewing as officers circled like vultures. But then, as quick as it came, the disbelief evaporated.

"Wait until my lawyer hears about this," she sneered, her green eyes narrowing into slits. She straightened her spine, molding her features into an expression of disdain. Composure became her shield, her thoughts already racing through scenarios, escape routes from this unforeseen trap.

Outside, the night erupted into a carnival of flashing lights and jostling bodies. Reporters swarmed, microphones thrust forward like spears, each eager for a slice of the scandal. Camera shutters clicked in rapid succession, capturing the drama unfolding at Sheila Chambers' doorstep.

"Was it all an act, Sheila?" a voice called out from the crowd. "How do you feel about being arrested for murder?"

"Smile for your fans!" another jeered, provocation laced with glee.

Sheila's lips curled into a smirk, a glint of satisfaction flickering across her face. Let them watch, she thought. She was a spectacle they couldn't look away from, and she reveled in it.

"Any words for Marlene's family?" a reporter pressed, pushing through the throng.

"Only that justice will prevail," Sheila answered, her tone dripping with a confidence she didn't fully feel. But doubt didn't suit her narrative—not now, not ever.

As the officers ushered her through the gauntlet of media, she held her head high. She was Sheila Chambers—cunning, ruthless, unbreakable. Or so she would have them believe.

The cuffs bit into Sheila's wrists as officers maneuvered her through the mob of reporters. Camera flashes ignited the night like staccato lightning, each burst punctuating the urgency of the moment. Questions hurled at her from every direction, voices clamoring over one another in a cacophony of curiosity and accusation.

"Who are you protecting, Sheila?"

"Did you act alone?"

"Is there anything you want to say?"

Sheila's lips twitched, the hint of a smirk dancing on the edge of defiance. Her eyes, still sharp with intellect, scanned the chaos—a general assessing the battlefield. She stepped forward, head held high, the very image of unyielding confidence. Reporters pushed against the line of police, their microphones outstretched, desperate for a soundbite from the woman at the heart of the storm.

"Justice is coming for you!" someone shouted from the back.

"Justice," Sheila echoed under her breath, the word a whisper of silk—smooth, cool, composed. It was her game now. They just didn't know it yet.

The rear door of the squad car swung open, and she slid into the backseat with practiced grace, despite the awkward angle of her handcuffed hands. The door slammed shut, severing her from the media's hungry gaze. Inside the vehicle, the world quieted to the murmur of radio chatter and the officers' measured breathing.

At the station, the atmosphere buzzed with a different kind of electricity. Officers bustled about, paperwork crinkling, keys jangling—a symphony of law and order at work. Sheila's red hair gleamed under the sterile fluorescent lights as they guided her to the booking area.

"Face the camera," an officer directed, his voice devoid of emotion.

Sheila turned, the ghost of a smile tracing her features. She didn't need words; her expression said it all. Defiant. Smug. Unrepentant. Photographer's bulbs flashed, capturing the image that would soon be etched into public memory: Sheila Chambers, the face of calculated cruelty, staring down the lens as if it were an old friend.

"Chin up, please," the officer instructed.

She complied, tilting her head ever so slightly. Control was her currency, and even now, she spent it wisely. Her piercing green eyes held the camera's gaze, an unspoken challenge lingering within their depths. This was her mugshot, but it might as well have been a portrait of triumph.

"Got it," the photographer said, stepping back. The click of the camera was a punctuation mark at the end of the sentence that had become Sheila Chambers' arrest.

"Good," Sheila murmured, almost to herself. "Make sure it's a good one."

Outside, the story of her capture was already rippling through the airwaves, igniting conversations in living rooms and bars. Sheila Chambers, enigmatic and dangerous, had finally been caught. But behind the smug façade captured in her mugshot, the gears of her mind whirred relentlessly. The game was far from over.

The photograph was everywhere. Sheila Chambers' face, smug and unrepentant, splashed across the morning headlines—broadcasted on TV screens, printed in newspapers, and shared on countless social media feeds. The public reeled at the sight, outrage pulsing through the city's veins like a toxin. This was the woman accused of tearing Marlene Thompson from her family, her community; this was the face behind the clown mask.

"Arrested," one headline screamed. "Justice for Marlene?" queried another. People shook their heads in disbelief, fingers pointing at the images as they sipped their coffee and muttered about the audacity of such a crime. Relief mingled with fury—the monster had a name, a face, and now, handcuffs.

Daniel Thompson stared at the screen, his mother's smile flashing in his mind—a stark contrast to Sheila's cold gaze. His throat tightened, fists clenched at his sides. Justice was a bitter word, tasting of grief and years lost. But this...this was a start.

"Son, you okay?" His father's voice was a lifeline in tumultuous seas.

"Seeing her face there—it's real now," Daniel rasped, eyes not leaving the screen. "She's caught."

"Marlene would be proud of you," his father said, voice thick with unshed tears. "You fought for this."

Grief crashed into Daniel anew, but it was tempered by a sliver of satisfaction. His mother's laughter echoed in his ears, a reminder of what was stolen, what he was fighting to honor. He nodded slowly, a silent vow passing between him and the image of the woman who stole so much.

"Let's see this through," Daniel murmured, more to himself than anyone else. "For mom."

The mugshot remained a fixture of the day, a constant reminder of the thin line between ordinary and evil. Daniel felt it, the weight of the world's shock and his own tempered relief, as he prepared for the next chapter of this long fight for justice.

Detective Brian Hayes leaned against the cold metal of his desk, the fluorescent lights above casting stark shadows across his face. Officer Jessica Lee stood beside him, her posture rigid, her eyes fixed on the screen displaying Sheila's mugshot—a trophy of their tireless pursuit.

"Long road, huh?" Hayes' voice was gravelly as he broke the silence that filled the precinct.

"Longer for some," Lee replied, thinking of Daniel Thompson and the years he'd waited for this moment.

"Marlene would've turned fifty next month," Hayes murmured, glancing at a photograph pinned to the corkboard—Marlene, forever frozen in time, smiling at a birthday party they'd never forget.

Lee nodded solemnly, "And Sheila? She'll be spending it in a cell."

"Should've been sooner. But evidence doesn't always play nice with timetables." Hayes' fingers drummed on the desk, betraying an impatience that mirrored his younger colleague's resolve.

"Doesn't matter now. We got her." Lee's statement was resolute, her faith in the justice system unshaken.

Hayes looked over at Lee, a flicker of admiration in his piercing blue eyes. "You did good, Officer. Marlene's case...it's personal for you."

"Isn't it for you?" she countered, her tone softening.

"Every case is personal. Some just hit closer to home." Hayes stood up straight, his stature commanding the room. "But this isn't over yet. Conviction's the real win."

"Challenges ahead," Lee acknowledged, her mind racing with the legal hurdles that awaited them.

"Plenty. Defense will claw at every shred of evidence we have." Hayes picked up the arrest report, the paper crinkling under his firm grip. "Sheila's smug. Thinks she's untouchable. We'll show her otherwise."

"By the book," Lee added, her gaze unwavering. "Every i dotted, every t crossed."

"Exactly. No shortcuts. Justice for Marlene, nothing less." Hayes' declaration hung in the air, a silent oath to see the trial through.

They shared a look of mutual respect, two warriors in a battle far from over. The chapter was closing, but the story—Sheila's trial, the quest for a conviction—was just beginning.

"Let's get to work," Hayes said finally, his tone imbued with the urgency that had become the heartbeat of the investigation.

"Right behind you, Detective," Lee affirmed, her steps matching his as they headed towards the door.

The precinct buzzed with activity around them, a hive of law enforcement driven by duty and the relentless pursuit of justice. And as they stepped out into the night, the promise of further developments loomed large, an anticipation that drove them forward, unwavering in their commitment to see justice served for Marlene.

The news vans had swarmed like vultures by dawn, satellite dishes pointing skyward as if to transmit the neighborhood's shock straight to the heavens. With Sheila Chambers' arrest, the once quiet street buzzed with a frenetic energy that bordered on hysteria.

"Can't believe it," one neighbor muttered into a reporter's microphone, eyes wide behind thick-rimmed glasses. "Sheila? She was always polite, you know? Quiet, kept to herself."

Another, an elderly man with a weathered face and hands deep in the pockets of his overalls, shook his head. "Thought I knew people," he said, voice barely rising above the clamor. "Guess not."

Camera shutters clicked incessantly, capturing every angle of Sheila's house – now a spectacle for public consumption. Reporters jostled for positions, their questions piercing the morning air with sharp intensity.

"Did she seem capable of this?" they prodded.

"Any odd behaviors you've noticed?"

"Could anyone have suspected?"

"Nothing," a woman replied, hugging her robe tighter around her. "Just... nothing out of the ordinary. It's chilling."

The community's disbelief was palpable, the air thick with confusion and the bitter tang of betrayal. Sheila, with her commanding presence and fiery hair, had been a fixture here, an ambitious figure climbing invisible runways. Now, her reputation lay in tatters, the pieces scattered across front pages and morning shows.

Detective Brian Hayes watched from a distance, noting the reactions, the collective denial. He understood their need to reconcile the image of the woman next door with the calculated criminal in the case file.

"Never saw it coming," he heard an acquaintance of Sheila's say, almost to himself. "She had edge, sure. But murder?"

Hayes exchanged a glance with Officer Jessica Lee, who stood beside him, arms crossed, her expression unreadable. They both knew the depth of Sheila's cunning, the cold strategy behind her green-eyed gaze. The neighbors were only now glimpsing the truth that had haunted the investigation.

"Media's eating this up," Lee commented, her voice steady despite the circus unfolding around them. "Gonna be a field day until the trial."

"Let 'em," Hayes replied curtly. "Focus is on the courtroom now. Public opinion doesn't decide her fate."

"Still," Lee said, shifting her weight, "it's part of the battle. Winning hearts and minds, shaping the narrative."

"True." Hayes nodded, turning away from the scene. "But our job's the same. Evidence. Facts. We build our case, piece by solid piece."

"Exactly," Lee agreed, following him back towards their unmarked car. "And we don't stop until justice is served."

The two detectives slipped away from the chaos, leaving the noise and the fervor behind. Their steps were measured, purposeful – each one a silent vow to keep digging, to keep fighting. For Marlene. For truth. For justice that would not be swayed by the court of public opinion.

Chapter 13

The defense attorney rose, a shark in the murky waters of reasonable doubt. "Ladies and gentlemen of the jury," he began, his voice steady but loaded with intent. He paced before them like a caged animal ready to pounce on the prosecution's case.

"DNA evidence," he said, pausing for effect. "It sounds definitive, doesn't it?" His eyes scanned the jurors, each one hanging onto his every word. "But is it infallible? The answer is a resounding no."

Sheila sat motionless, her green eyes locked onto the attorney. Each word he spoke was a step towards dismantling the web the prosecution had spun. Her red hair, usually so bright and fiery, lay subdued against the drab backdrop of the courtroom.

"Errors happen," the attorney continued. "Contamination is not just a possibility; it's a reality." He held up a photograph of the lab where the DNA analysis had been conducted. "In such an environment, a single mistake can turn an innocent person's life upside down."

He allowed the image to linger in the air, in their minds. Sheila watched as doubt crept into the furrows of the jurors' brows. They were beginning to see what she had known all along—that certainty was a luxury they couldn't afford in this trial.

"Think about it," the defense attorney urged, his tone sharpening like the blade of a knife. "A stray hair, a mislabeled sample, a moment of human error—it's all it takes to derail justice."

Sheila's lips curved, almost imperceptibly. It was that same cunning, that ruthless calculation she wielded so well, now being used in her favor. She didn't have to say a word; her attorney was her mouthpiece, casting the seeds of skepticism that would grow into her freedom.

"Beyond a reasonable doubt," he repeated, the phrase echoing through the courtroom like a drumbeat. "That's the standard we must uphold. And the DNA evidence? It simply doesn't meet that standard."

The attorney's words struck hard and fast, dismantling the prosecution's claims with the precision of a surgeon. Sheila remained still, but beneath the composed facade, her mind raced, analyzing each juror's reaction, each micro-expression of doubt. She was close, so very close to the verdict she desired.

The defense attorney paced before the jury, every step measured, deliberate. "And let's consider the chain of custody," he said, voice steady but charged with implication. "That sacred path from crime scene to courtroom."

Sheila watched him, a predator assessing her prey. She knew the importance of this moment — if the jury doubted the DNA, they doubted the case against her.

"Documents misplaced, protocols overlooked." He listed each misstep like a cardinal sin. "How can we trust evidence that may have been tainted?"

Jurors nodded, their faith wavering. Sheila's heart raced; she could almost hear the cogs turning in their heads.

"Moreover," the attorney went on, pausing for effect, "Ms. Chambers' hair in the getaway car." His gaze flicked to Sheila, who sat motionless, an enigma wrapped in red and green. "It tells us nothing definitive."

He let the words hang in the air, giving them weight, letting them sink into the minds of those who held Sheila's fate.

"Could be transfer. Could be coincidence." He shrugged, as if the very notion was too absurd to entertain. "Does not equate to murder."

Sheila's eyes darted between jurors, gauging their belief, feeding off their uncertainty. Her attorney was laying out the truth as she saw it — a fragmented puzzle, pieces forced together by a desperate prosecution.

"Remember," he implored, locking eyes with each juror, "reasonable doubt is your guide. Your compass."

Sheila remained still, but inside, her resolve solidified. She had always controlled the narrative, and now, once again, it was bending to her will.

The defense attorney leaned into the microphone, voice steady. "Ladies and gentlemen, consider alternative explanations." A hand swept through the air, a conductor cueing an orchestra. "Sheila Chambers' hair—could it not have found its way into that vehicle by innocent means?"

A murmur rippled through the courtroom. Jurors shifted in their seats, curiosity piqued.

"Or," he continued, his tone sharpening, "what if it was placed there by someone with a grudge? Someone wanting her out of the picture?" His eyes slid towards the prosecution table, a silent challenge.

Sheila's green gaze flickered. The faintest smile teased her lips. She knew about grudges, about the lengths people would go for revenge.

"Take Mr. Sam Miller, our costume shop clerk." The attorney's voice dipped, inviting the room into confidence. "An affable young man. Eager to please."

He paused, letting Sam's wholesome image settle before shattering it.

"Yet isn't it true that behind that friendly exterior could lurk other motives?" He peered at the jury, as if sharing a secret. "Could his testimony be tainted by personal bias against Ms. Chambers?"

Sam squirmed on the witness stand, his boyish face clouding over. Sheila watched him, unblinking. Her red hair, vibrant against the sterile courtroom, was a banner of defiance.

"Is it not possible," the attorney pressed on, relentless, "that Mr. Miller saw an opportunity to pin a crime on someone else?" His words jabbed at the jury, puncturing holes in the prosecution's narrative.

"Reasonable doubt," he hammered the point home, "it surrounds us."

Sheila sat back, her posture relaxed but commanding. The room's energy crackled, every eye on her, every mind churning with the what-ifs her attorney had unleashed.

The defense attorney turned from the jury, a nod to Sheila. It was all unfolding as planned. They weren't just casting doubt; they were rewriting the story.

And Sheila, she thrived on rewritten stories.

The attorney paced before the jury, a predator in pinstripes. "Witness testimony," he said with a measured tone that belied the intensity of his gaze. "It's powerful, yes. Persuasive, certainly." He stopped, hands clasping behind his back as he faced the twelve jurors head-on. "But is it enough to condemn a woman to a life behind bars? Is it enough when there's no direct evidence tying her to the murder weapon? To the crime scene?"

Sheila watched from the defense table, her piercing green eyes tracking the attorney's every move. The muscles in her jaw clenched then relaxed, betraying nothing of her inner turmoil.

"Consider this," the attorney continued, voice rising slightly, quick and sharp. "No fingerprints. No bloodstains. No video footage. Just words. Words from individuals who may have their own reasons for weaving tales."

A juror shifted, uncomfortable. Another scribbled notes, pen scratching paper in the thick silence. They felt it—the weight of doubt settling like fog.

"Reasonable doubt," the attorney said, turning to face the jury squarely, his voice now infused with urgency. "It's not just a standard; it's the cornerstone of justice."

Sheila remained still, a statue carved from ice and strategy. Her red hair was a stark contrast against the drab courtroom, a splash of color in a sea of grey morality.

"Is Sheila Chambers guilty beyond a reasonable doubt?" The attorney's question hung in the air, echoing off the walls. "Or is she a victim of circumstance? Of conjecture and coincidence?"

The jurors were listening, really listening. The seeds of skepticism had been sown. Now they needed only to take root.

"Every piece of evidence should be a thread in a tapestry of truth," the attorney said, circling like a shark scenting blood. "But what does it mean if those threads don't connect? What does it mean if the tapestry is incomplete?"

Sheila's heart raced, though her expression remained impassive. This was the crux of it all. The moment when the scales could tip, when freedom or incarceration hung in the balance.

"Your decision," the attorney implored, locking eyes with each member of the jury, "must be based on certainties, not possibilities. On evidence, not assumptions."

The room was charged with the electricity of minds at work, thoughts churning, doubts growing. The prosecution watched, stone-faced, knowing their case wavered on the precipice of reasonable doubt.

"Remember," the attorney concluded, voice resonating with conviction, "without direct evidence, without undeniable proof, you cannot—must not—find Sheila Chambers guilty."

Sheila's gaze swept across the courtroom one final time, her future dangling on the precipice of the jury's conscience.

Sheila Chambers sat rigid, a statue of restraint. Her hands folded neatly in her lap, not a single red strand out of place. But beneath the surface, turmoil churned like a tempest. The trial had etched lines of strain around her piercing green eyes, usually so sharp and calculating. Now they betrayed a glimmer of something raw, something human.

"Let's consider for a moment," the defense attorney stated, voice clear and concise, "the human cost of this trial." His gaze lingered on Sheila, then swept over the jury. "This woman before you has endured months of public scrutiny, her life dissected under a microscope, her character assassinated in the court of public opinion."

A juror shifted uncomfortably. Another dabbed at her eye.

"An investigation," he continued, "that should have been thorough and unbiased, yet was anything but." He paced slowly, each step measured, deliberate. "A rush to judgment that has left Ms. Chambers fighting not just for her freedom but for her very identity."

The courtroom was silent save for the quiet creak of a chair, the scratch of a pen. Sheila remained motionless, but inside, the words ignited a flicker of hope.

"Presumption of innocence," the attorney said, turning back to face the jurors, "is the bedrock of our legal system." His tone hardened, underscored by the gravity of his words. "It is not simply a legal principle. It is a promise. A promise that every person stands innocent until proven guilty beyond a reasonable doubt."

Jurors nodded, the weight of their responsibility evident in their furrowed brows.

"Has the prosecution met this burden?" He let the question hang in the air, heavy with implication.

Sheila's heart hammered in her chest, her composure a carefully maintained facade. She knew all too well the stakes of this gamble, the razor-thin line between victory and downfall.

"The evidence against Ms. Chambers," the attorney declared, "is circumstantial at best, dubious at worst. You must ask yourselves—is this enough to shatter a life? Is this enough to send an innocent person to prison?"

No sound dared intrude upon his final words.

"Your verdict holds power. Power to correct an injustice, to uphold the integrity of our justice system. I trust you will wield it with wisdom and courage."

Eyes locked on the jury, the defense attorney stepped back, his case laid bare. Sheila's fate now rested in their hands. She let out a breath she didn't realize she'd been holding, her green eyes seeking truth in a sea of faces.

The courtroom buzzed, a hive of whispers and shifting papers. At the prosecution table, a silent exchange unfolded. Detective Brian Hayes caught the eye of Officer Jessica Lee, a single brow arched in concern. Her return glance spoke volumes; they both sensed it—the defense had left an indelible mark on the jury's mind.

Brian's jaw set firm, his hands folded neatly atop the stack of evidence folders that now seemed less concrete than mere hours ago. Each piece, once a sturdy brick in their wall of accusation, now felt like a precarious stone, teetering at the edge of collapse.

Jessica shifted in her seat, the fabric of her uniform rustling softly. The doubt was palpable, a specter haunting their confidence. She glanced at her notes, the scrawled observations and meticulous records she'd kept. They were thorough, detailed, but suddenly, under the scrutiny of the defense's narrative, they appeared to her as fragile threads in a vast tapestry of what-ifs.

A sharp rap from the judge's gavel sliced through the murmur, demanding attention. "Ladies and gentlemen," the judge intoned, his voice echoing off the high ceilings. Every pair of eyes swiveled toward the bench, where authority resided in black robes and stern gazes.

"Please listen carefully to the following instructions." The words were routine, but their significance loomed large, heavy with the power to decide Sheila's fate. Jurors leaned forward, eager for guidance, while Sheila sat frozen, a statue carved from tension and anticipation.

"Your duty is to weigh the evidence," the judge continued. The room held its breath. "You must determine whether the prosecution has proven the defendant's guilt beyond a reasonable doubt."

Brian's gaze lingered on the jury, their faces mosaic tiles of thought and emotion. Some scribbled notes, others merely listened, each processing the gravity of their task. He knew them by name, by occupation, by the little tells they'd shown throughout the trial. Now, they were inscrutable, veiled by the solemnity of their charge.

"Disregard any emotion or sympathy," the judge admonished. The command was clear, the expectation set. Facts over feelings, evidence over empathy.

The clock ticked. Seconds became minutes. Each moment dragged, laden with consequence. The air in the courtroom thickened, a tangible pressure that pressed against walls lined with legal tomes and portraits of justice.

Brian could feel the verdict hanging in the balance, a sword suspended by the slenderest thread. Beside him, Jessica tensed, her pen poised above the notepad, as if ready to spring into action at a moment's notice. But there was nothing more for them to do, no further argument to present, no last-minute evidence to unveil.

As the judge's instructions drew to a close, the jurors filed out, a procession marked by the weight of the world upon their shoulders. The door closed behind them with a click that resonated like a gavel's final word.

Silence swelled in their absence, a void filled with unspoken fears and unvoiced hopes. In that stillness, the future of Sheila Chambers hung precariously—a pendulum whose swing would soon reveal a destiny written in the ink of law and etched by the hand of justice.

Sheila Chambers sat statue-still, her back rigid against the unforgiving wooden bench. A veneer of calm masked the turmoil churning within. Her piercing green eyes swept across the courtroom—a sea of faces blurring into one indistinct judgment. She cataloged each person, a silent observer playing her role to perfection.

Her mind raced, replaying the trial's twists and turns. The defense had been cunning, meticulous. But was it enough? The prosecution's case, once ironclad, now seemed riddled with holes—holes she had carefully helped to pry open.

The courtroom's hush felt like the quiet before a storm. Sheila's heart thumped, a relentless drumbeat echoing in her ears. She could almost hear the jurors deliberating, their words slicing through her future with every passing second.

She fixed her gaze on the jury room door, willing it to swing open, to end the excruciating wait. Time was a cruel adversary; it slowed to a crawl when she most wished it to sprint.

Detective Hayes and Officer Lee were statues in their own right. They too waited, their careers momentarily tethered to the twelve minds deliberating beyond the oak barrier. Their earlier exchange of glances had not escaped her notice. Doubt had crept into their certainty, fear into their confidence.

The judge shuffled papers, a sound impossibly loud in the silence. Sheila's attorney offered her a reassuring nod. She returned it with a measured smile, her expression unyielding, unreadable.

To the world, she was an enigma—a puzzle yet unsolved. To herself, she was the master of her fate, the architect of her destiny. But the power to decide lay just out of reach, in the hands of others.

Sheila's eyes remained locked on the door. Any moment now, the knob could turn, the hinges could creak. Any moment could shatter the stillness, usher in her future or herald her downfall.

Then, a faint noise—a cough from the corridor. Sheila tensed. Was this it?

The courtroom held its breath.

And the door stayed closed.

Chapter 14

Brian's fingers drummed a staccato rhythm on the edge of the evidence board, his gaze sweeping over every item pinned to its surface. Jessica stood beside him, her arms crossed tight across her chest as she leaned in, scrutinizing the photos and documents that formed a web of connections—all leading to Sheila Chambers. The red strings crisscrossed like veins, but the heart of the matter, the link to the murder weapon and crime scene, was conspicuously absent.

"Anything?" Brian's gruff voice broke the tense silence.

"Nothing new," Jessica replied, her tone tight with frustration. "We're missing something—something critical."

Brian nodded, his jaw set firm. He had seen cases go cold for less. His eyes locked onto a grainy surveillance photo of Sheila, her red hair a fiery marker in the black-and-white image. She was there, somewhere in the puzzle, but how?

"We revisit the crime scene," he decided abruptly. "Now."

Jessica's eyes flashed with renewed vigor. "Let's do it."

They moved swiftly out of the station, their minds racing ahead to the shadowed alley where Marlene's life was brutally snatched away. As they drove, Brian's hands gripped the steering wheel with purpose, each turn bringing them closer to the answers they so desperately needed. Jessica reviewed the case file, her finger tracing the route Sheila could have taken that fateful night.

"Every case cracks open with one overlooked detail," Brian muttered, more to himself than to Jessica. "We find it."

"Agreed," Jessica said, determination etched into every word. "She won't get away with this."

The car came to a halt at the mouth of the alley, the scene was quiet now, a stark contrast to the chaos of the investigation's early days. They stepped out, their senses heightened, searching for anything amiss. Every discarded piece of trash, every smudge on the walls was a potential clue calling out to be discovered.

"Start from the beginning," Brian instructed, his blue eyes scanning the area with methodical precision. "Every step she took, we take."

"Got it," Jessica confirmed, moving ahead to follow the ghost of Sheila's trail.

Together, they combed through the alley, their presence a silent challenge to the secrets hidden within its confines. Every shadow was inspected, every possible witness's memory would be tapped. Brian and Jessica were determined to unearth the truth, no matter how deeply it was buried. With every fiber of their being focused on the task, the hunt for justice pushed them forward relentlessly.

Jessica's fingers drummed a rapid beat on the steering wheel as she pressed the phone to her ear, her gaze locked on the crime scene tape fluttering in the distance. "Any updates?" she asked, voice taut with anticipation.

"Nothing new," came the reply from the forensic analyst on the other end. "We're still running the tests, but no breakthroughs yet."

Her hand clenched the phone tighter, frustration simmering. "Keep me posted," she said curtly before ending the call.

"Damn it," she muttered under her breath, the lack of progress gnawing at her.

Brian caught the edge in her voice and turned to face her, his own expression a mirror of her vexation. "What's our next move?" he asked, his words clipped and decisive.

"We need something concrete," Jessica said, eyes narrowing as her mind raced. "A direct connection to Sheila—fingerprints, DNA, anything on that murder weapon."

"Or a confession," Brian added, his jaw set. "But we both know Sheila's too clever for a misstep like that."

"Then we outsmart her," Jessica declared, her resolve hardening. "We find what links her to the crime. A thread, a whisper, something she overlooked."

Brian nodded, his blue eyes sharp with the same intensity. "We go back through everything. Every interview, every alibi. She's hiding something; it's up to us to uncover it."

"Let's dig deeper into her past," Jessica suggested, flipping open her notebook. "There must be patterns, behaviors... clues that point to this moment."

"Agreed." Brian leaned in closer, their heads almost touching as they poured over the notes. "She's ambitious, ruthless. There has to be a trail of stepping stones leading up to this."

"Maybe she needed Marlene out of the picture for a reason tied to her job, or her climb up the ladder," Jessica mused, her finger tracing lines between the facts.

"Or personal vendetta," Brian offered, his voice low and steady. "Either way, we find the link."

Their determination was palpable in the car's confined space as they pieced together theories, each possibility a potential key to unlocking the truth. The urgency of their mission left no room for doubt—they would catch Sheila Chambers, one way or another.

Brian swept a hand across the scattered photos, his gaze flicking from one image to the next. "We need more eyes," he said curtly.

"Exactly." Jessica's fingers danced over the keyboard. "I'll pull up the witness list again. Someone must have seen Sheila that day."

"Start with the locals," Brian instructed as Jessica's ponytail bobbed in agreement, her brown eyes scanning the database with fervor. "Shopkeepers, street vendors—the sort who notice when things are out of place."

"Got it." She started making calls, her voice a steady drumbeat of inquiries. Each call ended with notes scribbled furiously onto a pad—times, descriptions, the faintest recollections of a woman with fiery hair.

"Anything?" Brian's voice cut through the rhythm of Jessica's work.

"Maybe," she replied. "A barista remembers a red-haired woman arguing on the phone outside the coffee shop that morning."

"Good. What else?"

"Still digging." Her resolve was an unspoken undercurrent in her tone.

Brian turned to his own phone, thumbing through contacts until he found the names he needed. Old partners, seasoned detectives who had seen their fair share of cunning perpetrators. He dialed the first number, the beeps quick and decisive.

"Mike, it's Hayes." His words were clipped. "Got a minute?"

The murmur of a response, then Brian was outlining the case, his tone all business. He listened intently, nodding even though the person on the other end couldn't see.

"Right. No, we've considered that" A pause. "Yeah, I'll tell her to check."

He hung up, turning to Jessica. "Cross-reference Sheila's credit card statements. Mike says to look for patterns, anything repetitive or out of place."

"Doing it now," Jessica confirmed, her fingers already flying over keys. The screen before her flickered with transaction histories.

"Reach out to Stan and Rita too," he added. "They might remember a similar MO from back in the day."

"Will do." Jessica didn't miss a beat. "If Sheila slipped up, we'll find it."

"Stay sharp," Brian encouraged, his blue eyes intense. "She's smart, but everyone makes mistakes."

"Let's hope she made hers," Jessica muttered, determination etched in her every move as they continued their relentless search against the ticking clock of justice.

Jessica jabbed the phone's speaker button with a bit more force than necessary. The lab's hold music, a grating loop of synthesized strings, filled the cramped office. Brian glanced up from the spread of documents, an eyebrow raised in silent question.

"Still waiting," she mouthed, her frustration palpable.

"Lee here. Any news on the DNA samples from the getaway car?" Her voice held an edge, the kind that came from too many late nights chasing ghosts in the evidence.

"Officer Lee, we're processing as fast as we can, but—" The lab technician's voice was apologetic, yet it did nothing to soothe Jessica's impatience.

"Look, I need something, anything. We're at a dead end here." She drummed her fingers on the desk, each tap a second ticking by without answers.

"Understood. I'll push your request to the top of the list. I'll call you the moment we have results," the technician promised before the line went dead.

"Great. More waiting," Jessica muttered, disconnecting the call.

"Patience, Lee. The evidence will come," Brian said, though his own expression betrayed a similar urgency. He returned his focus to the papers scattered before them, witness statements and interview transcripts that formed a maze of words and potential leads.

"Let's go over these again. From the top," he instructed, picking up the first statement. His finger slid along the lines of text as he read, blue eyes darting back and forth, searching for the slightest crack in the narrative.

"Here," Jessica leaned forward, pointing to a paragraph in one of the transcripts. "This witness saw a woman matching Sheila's description, but look at the time stamp. It doesn't add up."

"Good catch," Brian acknowledged, making a note in the margin. "Could be a mistake, but let's keep digging."

They sifted through pages, cross-referencing times, locations, descriptions. Each piece of testimony was scrutinized, dissected under their combined gaze. Jessica's earlier restlessness shifted into a laser-focused attention to detail, mirroring Brian's methodical approach.

"Nothing here contradicts our timeline," Brian concluded after they had revisited the last of the interviews. "But it doesn't get us closer to Sheila either."

"Someone has to have seen something. We're missing a piece of the puzzle," Jessica said, her tone resolute despite the lack of progress. "We'll find it."

"Agreed. No stone unturned," Brian echoed, stacking the papers neatly. His movements were precise, betraying none of the frustration that gnawed at him. "Sheila's out there, thinking she's covered her tracks. It's our job to prove her wrong."

"Exactly." Jessica stood, stretching her back. "Let's circle back to the crime scene tomorrow, fresh eyes might spot something new."

"First light," Brian confirmed with a nod. "Rest up, Lee. Tomorrow, we break this case wide open."

As night settled over the city, the two officers steeled themselves for the challenge ahead. The truth was hidden within the tangle of evidence and alibis, but one thing was certain – they wouldn't stop until justice was served.

Jessica clicked away at the keyboard, her brow furrowed in concentration. "If Sheila's involved, it's got to be for a reason," she muttered. Her fingers danced across the keys, pulling up financial records, bank statements, anything that could hint at a motive.

"Money trails don't lie," Brian said, peering over her shoulder.

"Exactly." She zoomed in on a series of transactions, her finger tapping rapidly on the screen. "Look at this—large cash deposits, way above her pay grade."

"Could be our missing link," Brian acknowledged, his voice low but hopeful.

"Or someone's paying her silence." Jessica's eyes were sharp, analytical. "We need to dig deeper into these connections."

"Let's chart out her associates," Brian suggested, pulling up a blank digital board. They began mapping out names and relationships, a web of potential allies and conspiracies forming before them.

Meanwhile, Brian's phone buzzed with urgency. He picked it up, glancing at the caller ID before putting it on speaker. "Hayes," he answered.

"District Attorney's office, returning your call," came the brisk voice on the other end.

"Thanks for getting back to me." Brian didn't waste words. "We're considering a plea deal for any accomplices willing to talk about Sheila Chambers."

"Risky without hard evidence," the DA cautioned.

"We believe someone out there can tie her to the crime scene," Brian insisted. "We just need to shake the tree."

"Understood," the DA replied. "I'll draft something tentative. Keep me posted."

"Will do," Brian said before ending the call. He looked at Jessica. "Time to start shaking."

"Got it." Jessica's reply was curt, her focus unbroken as she dove back into the sea of data. Every click, every scrolled page brought them closer to the truth they sought.

"Let's turn the heat up on Sheila's circle," Jessica said, determination lacing her words. "Someone's bound to crack."

"Agreed," Brian responded. They shared a resolute nod, their resolve as strong as the coffee growing cold beside them.

Jessica rapped softly on Daniel's door. It swung open, revealing a young man with dark circles under his eyes and a face etched with grief. She stepped into the dimly lit living room, her presence a somber reminder of the world outside his sorrow.

"Officer Lee," Daniel murmured, his voice hoarse.

"Daniel." Her tone was gentle, respectful. "I wanted to update you personally."

He nodded, sinking onto an old couch that had seen better days. She sat beside him, close enough to offer comfort, yet giving space for his pain.

"We're pushing hard on this case," Jessica began, her eyes meeting his. The determined brown orbs held a promise. "Sheila Chambers is at the heart of our investigation."

"Any... any new evidence?" His words were hopeful, but his posture slumped in anticipation of disappointment.

"Still working through it," she admitted. "But we won't rest until we've turned over every stone."

"Thank you," he whispered, clutching a frayed photograph of Marlene. "Mom deserves justice."

Jessica reached out, placing a reassuring hand on his shoulder. "We'll find it, Daniel. We owe her that much."

A silent understanding passed between them before Jessica stood, leaving Daniel with his memories and a renewed sense of determination fueling her resolve.

*****

Back at the precinct, Brian was waiting, his gaze locked on a cluster of forensic reports scattered across the table. The fluorescent lights hummed overhead, casting stark shadows against the walls lined with evidence.

"Got anything?" Jessica asked, sliding into the chair opposite him.

"Maybe," Brian grunted, tapping a finger on a lab report. "We need a different angle on these samples."

"Alternative methods?" Jessica's brow furrowed as she leaned in, scanning the documents.

"Exactly." Brian's blue eyes met hers, a spark of shared tenacity igniting between them. "We talk to the forensic team, see what they can do with what we've got."

Minutes later, they stood side by side in the sterile confines of the forensics lab. Beakers clinked, machines whirred—a symphony of science at work.

"Dr. Keller," Brian greeted the lead forensic analyst, a woman whose keen intellect was matched only by her meticulous nature.

"Detective Hayes, Officer Lee," Dr. Keller acknowledged, removing her glasses. "What brings you down here?"

"Looking for creative solutions," Jessica said, her tone direct. "The samples from the getaway car—"

"Need more than the usual tests," Brian finished, his expression earnest.

"Understood," Dr. Keller nodded, considering the challenge. "We might try amplifying degraded DNA, or perhaps trace analysis for environmental markers."

"Anything that could tie Sheila to the scene," Jessica added, the urgency clear in her voice.

"Let me pull my team together," Dr. Keller decided, slipping her glasses back on. "We'll brainstorm and run some trials."

"Appreciate it, Doctor," Brian said, offering a grateful nod.

"Time's not on our side," Jessica reminded them all, her gaze unwavering. "We need a breakthrough."

"Leave it to us," Dr. Keller assured, turning back to her instruments of truth.

Brian and Jessica exited the lab, their footsteps echoing down the corridor, each step a testament to their relentless pursuit. They shared a look of steely conviction, knowing that somewhere within the fibers and fluids lay the key to unlocking the justice Marlene deserved.

The precinct was a hive of activity, but in the corner office, time seemed to slow. Jessica pored over Sheila's file, her fingers tracing the timeline of a life spent skirting the edges of legality. "Look at this," she called out, tapping on a report. "Sheila jumped jobs like checkers—always one step ahead of trouble."

"Any patterns?" Brian asked, leaning over her shoulder, his eyes scanning the records.

"Always places with access—" Jessica paused, realization dawning, "—access to potential victims or accomplices."

"Dig deeper," Brian urged, his voice low and steady. "We need something solid."

Together, they combed through Sheila's history, unearthing connections and questioning coincidences. Each detail meticulously noted, each lead followed with dogged precision.

"Time for the footage," Brian decided, shifting gears. They moved to the monitors, where hours of video awaited their scrutiny.

"Could be our best chance at placing her at the scene," Jessica acknowledged, her gaze fixed on the grainy images flickering across the screen.

They watched, rewound, and rewatched. The monotonous hum of the machines provided a backdrop to their silent concentration. Brian's finger hovered over the controls, pausing on a frame, zooming in, seeking the truth hidden in plain sight.

"Wait," Jessica said suddenly, her voice cutting through the rhythm of their routine. "There—enhance that segment."

Brian obliged, enlarging the image. A figure, red hair unmistakable even in black and white, moved across the screen.

"Got you," Brian muttered under his breath, a small victory in an ocean of uncertainty.

"Timestamp it," Jessica instructed, already reaching for the phone. "That's within the window of opportunity."

"Good catch, Lee," Brian acknowledged, nodularity in his tone. They had a piece of the puzzle now, a piece that could very well fit into the gaping hole of their case against Sheila Chambers.

Their determination burned brighter, fueled by the prospect of justice within reach. With every second that passed, they drew closer to the answers they sought. The hunt continued, relentless and unyielding.

Jessica jabbed the call button, her thumb pressing hard against the phone's worn surface. She held the receiver tight to her ear, pacing the length of the cluttered office. The incessant ringing mocked her urgency—each tone amplifying her frustration.

"Forensics," a voice finally answered.

"Lee here. I need an update on the DNA samples from the clown car. It's critical," she said, her voice sharp, commanding.

"Officer Lee, we're swamped. No news yet."

"Listen," Jessica pressed, "Sheila Chambers' entire case hinges on this. I need those results. Prioritize them."

"We'll do our best, but—"

"Best isn't good enough." Jessica cut him off, her impatience a live wire. "Push it through. Call me the minute you have something."

The line clicked dead, leaving Jessica seething in silence. Her gaze met Brian's across the room, his raised eyebrows acknowledging the tension.

"Forensics is dragging their feet," she explained, her hands making fists at her sides.

Brian nodded slowly, the lines on his forehead deepening. "We can't afford delays. If Sheila walks..."

He didn't need to finish. They knew the stakes.

"Marlene's family is counting on us," Jessica said, her brown eyes dark with resolve. "The community needs closure. We can't let a killer roam free."

"Justice has a clock," Brian added gravely, his blue eyes meeting hers. "And time is ticking against us."

"Then we work faster, dig deeper. Whatever it takes," Jessica declared, her ponytail swinging as she turned back to the evidence board. "She won't walk, Brian. Not on our watch."

Brian's lips pressed into a thin line, the barest hint of a nod. Together, they stood, guardians of justice, ready to battle time itself to bring a murderer to heel.

Jessica's fingers flew across the keyboard, the click-clack of keys punctuating the charged silence. She was casting a digital net, emails and requests shooting out to every law enforcement database she could access. "There's got to be something," she muttered, her eyes scanning the screen for case files on clown-related crimes or peculiar murder weapons.

"Check circus troupes, traveling performers. Hell, look up professional clowns' forums if you have to," Brian suggested, leaning over her shoulder. His voice carried the weight of years spent combing through the darker corners of humanity.

"Already on it," Jessica responded without looking up. She opened tabs upon tabs, her searches branching out like tendrils seeking sunlight. Reports filtered in, a deluge of data that held potential keys to Sheila's downfall. Each notification was a heartbeat, a pulse of hope.

"Send out feelers to the FBI behavioral units, too," Brian said, his tone sharpening with focus. "They might have profiles that fit Sheila's M.O."

"Good call." Jessica nodded, tapping into federal resources. Her request was simple and urgent: Any intel on individuals using clown disguises for criminal activities? Anything unusual, unorthodox?

As data streamed in, Brian pulled out Sheila's alibi statement, spreading it across the desk like a map to be deciphered. His eyes, sharp as flint, began dissecting each word, each claimed timestamp. "We need to punch holes in this," he said with grim determination.

"Let's cross-reference," Jessica said, pivoting from her online search to join him. Together, they pored over surveillance footage timelines, credit card receipts, cell tower pings—all the pieces of Sheila's carefully constructed narrative.

"Here," Jessica pointed at a line in the transcript. "She says she was at the diner, but the waitress doesn't remember seeing her that night."

"Get the traffic cams. Check for her car," Brian directed, his finger tracing the route Sheila would have taken. They were hunters, tracking their prey through the dense forest of lies and half-truths.

"Got a hit!" Jessica's exclamation sliced through the tension. A camera had caught a glimpse of Sheila's car, but not near the diner—closer to the crime scene, at a critical time. A bead of sweat trailed down Brian's temple as he leaned in closer.

"Print that out. We'll add it to our timeline," he said, his voice steady but electric with implication. This was it—a crack in Sheila's armor.

"Anything else?" Jessica asked, her eyes fierce with anticipation.

"Keep digging," Brian replied, his resolve echoing hers. "Every detail matters."

"Until we break her story wide open," Jessica finished, her gaze returning to the screen, ready to unearth the next shattering truth.

Jessica jabbed at the phone's keypad, her movements sharp and efficient. She held the receiver tight to her ear, pacing the cramped confines of the evidence room. The air was stale, thick with the scent of old paper and cold coffee, but she barely noticed—her focus was laser-sharp on the voice that crackled through the line.

"Listen, I need those results," she pressed, her tone clipped and insistent. "We're running against the clock here. Can you push it through? Anything to give us an edge."

The lab tech on the other end hesitated before responding, his words slow and apologetic. No progress, no breakthroughs—just the same bureaucratic delays. Jessica's grip tightened, knuckles whitening, a physical manifestation of her mounting frustration.

"Understand we can't just sit on our hands!" Her voice rose, echoing off the walls. "This isn't about procedure; it's about justice. Marlene deserves that much."

She slammed down the receiver, the click as final as a judge's gavel. Turning, she caught Brian's eye. He'd been watching her, his seasoned gaze taking in every nuance of the exchange. They were both feeling it—the pressure, the urgency, the unspoken dread of what might happen if they failed.

"Dammit, Brian. We need something concrete or she walks," Jessica spat out, her brown eyes blazing with a fire that matched her words.

Brian pushed away from the table, every line in his face etched with resolve. "She won't walk. Not on my watch." His voice was gravel, toughened by years of battles just like this one.

"Her walking means we didn't do enough. It means doubt creeps into every corner of this department. Our credibility..." Jessica's voice trailed off, the implications hanging heavy between them.

"Look, Jess," Brian said, stepping closer, "I've seen cases go south, seen the fallout. We can't let that fear paralyze us. We use it. We work harder, dig deeper, fight smarter."

Jessica nodded, steeling herself. "So we throw everything we have at this. Witnesses, surveillance, DNA—everything."

"Everything," Brian echoed.

"Because if she walks..." Jessica began.

"Then we didn't just fail Marlene," Brian finished for her, "we failed ourselves, the badge, and this entire city. And that," he paused, his blue eyes fierce, "is not an option."

Together, in silent agreement, they turned back to the evidence board. Photos, timelines, witness statements—all the scattered pieces of a puzzle they were determined to solve. Their shared commitment hung palpable in the air, a promise made not just to each other, but to the very essence of the justice they both served.

Chapter 15

Sam Miller's fingers fumbled for the microphone, a slight quiver betraying his nerves. He raised it inch by careful inch, locking it into place as he exhaled slowly. His eyes swept over the courtroom's expectant gaze, settling on the solemn duty that awaited him.

"Please state your name and occupation for the record," the Prosecution attorney said, approaching with measured steps.

"Samuel Miller, I work at Henderson's Costume Shop," he replied, voice steadier than his hands.

"Mr. Miller, how long have you been employed at this costume shop?"

"Three years," Sam asserted, pushing his glasses up the bridge of his nose.

"And in those three years, would you say you've become quite familiar with the inventory?"

"Absolutely. I know it inside out," he said, confidence creeping into his tone.

"Your job requires you to interact with customers daily, correct?"

"Yes, sir."

"Would you describe yourself as having a good memory for faces, Mr. Miller?"

"I would, yes." Sam leaned forward slightly, eager to affirm his reliability.

"Thank you. Your expertise in costume types and customer interactions is crucial here," the attorney nodded, flipping through a stack of notes. "Now, let's delve into the specifics of your encounter on the day in question."

"Mr. Miller, can you identify the individual who purchased the clown outfit in question?" The Prosecution attorney's voice cut through the courtroom's tense silence.

Sam's gaze shifted decisively across the room, locking onto the figure seated at the defense table. "Yes," he said, his words firm, unyielding. He raised an arm, pointing directly at the defendant. "That's her. Sheila Chambers."

Whispers fluttered like disturbed pigeons among the spectators. Sheila remained motionless, her piercing green eyes fixed on Sam, as if daring him to falter.

"Let the record show that the witness has identified Ms. Chambers," the judge announced, scribbling a note.

The Defense attorney rose, the fabric of his suit whispering against the leather chair. His approach was predatory, a calculated move to unsettle the young man on the stand.

"Mr. Miller," he began, his tone laced with skepticism, "you see many customers every day, do you not?"

"I do," Sam acknowledged, but his voice did not waver.

"And yet you claim to remember Ms. Chambers distinctly, out of the countless individuals you encounter?"

"Distinctly," Sam reaffirmed, meeting the attorney's probing stare without hesitation.

"Interesting." The word hung heavy, implying doubt. "Is it not possible, Mr. Miller, that you could have mistaken my client for someone else? Human memory is notoriously unreliable, after all."

Sam's fingers tightened imperceptibly around the edge of the stand, but his reply came as calmly as ever. "Not in this case. Some customers stand out. Sheila Chambers is one of them."

"Stand out, you say?" The Defense attorney's eyebrow arched, a silent challenge thrown down before the court.

"Absolutely," Sam pressed on, his resolve a testament to the truth he carried. The theatrical flair of his dialogue style had no place here; only the stark, unembellished reality of what he knew. "She was... memorable."

"Memorable," echoed the attorney, each syllable weighed with implication. Yet, despite his efforts, the certainty in Sam's eyes remained unshaken—a beacon of unwavering confidence amidst a sea of doubt.

Sam straightened his posture, the tremor in his hands stilled. His gaze settled on the Prosecution attorney as he prepared to delve into the particulars of that day. "She insisted on paying with cash," he stated. "Five hundred-dollar bills. No credit card, no check."

"Unusual?" asked the attorney, leaning forward.

"Very." Sam nodded. "Most customers use cards. It's easier to track. Safer."

"Her demeanor?" The question hung in the air, demanding precision.

"Excited," Sam replied. "More than excited—almost... giddy."

"Giddy," echoed the attorney, scribbling a note.

"Like a kid in a candy store," Sam elaborated, recalling the intensity in Sheila's piercing green eyes, the way her red hair seemed to shimmer with anticipation. Her bold energy had been out of place amidst the aisles of costumes and props.

"Any specific comments she made during this transaction?" The attorney's voice cut through the courtroom's silence.

Sam paused, replaying the moment in his mind like a scene from one of his plays. "She said she didn't need a bag. Wanted to wear it out of the store."

"Anything else?"

He hesitated, not for lack of memory but for the weight of what he was about to reveal. "She mentioned... not needing a receipt. Said she wouldn't be returning it."

"Thank you, Mr. Miller." The Prosecution attorney gave a nod of approval before turning back to the judge, confident in the testimony's impact.

Sam felt a silent rush of adrenaline. His words, sharp and clear, had painted the picture, each detail a stroke of truth against the canvas of justice.

Sam's mind flickered back to the day of purchase, Sheila's words echoing with a biting edge. "It's for a special occasion," she had sneered, the sarcasm dripping from her tongue like venom. She waved off his offer of a receipt with a casual flick of her wrist, her green eyes alight with a cold fire.

"Who needs it?" Sheila had scoffed at the mention of the shop's return policy. "This is a one-time show."

The courtroom hushed as Sam recounted the interaction, the memory etched into his consciousness. The lack of concern for leaving a paper trail was blatant, intentional.

"Thank you, Mr. Miller," the Prosecution attorney said, satisfied.

The Defense attorney stood, sharp and predatory. He prowled toward Sam, a glint of challenge in his eyes. "Mr. Miller, isn't it true that you could hold a grudge against my client?" His voice, slick with insinuation, filled the room.

"Objection!" The Prosecution attorney's objection was swift.

"Overruled. Answer the question," the judge instructed, his gaze fixed on Sam.

"No grudge," Sam replied, his tone steady. "Just the facts."

"Is it not a fact that you're an actor?" The Defense attorney's question came rapid-fire. "A storyteller by trade?"

Sam nodded, unfazed. "I work at the costume shop. Acting is my passion, not my profession."

"Convenient." The attorney's smile was thin, unkind. "A flair for the dramatic, perhaps an embellishment here or there?"

"Objection, Your Honor. Counsel is badgering the witness," the Prosecution attorney interjected.

"Let's keep to the facts," the judge warned, silencing the objections with a firm hand.

"Of course, Your Honor," the Defense attorney conceded, though his stance remained aggressive.

"Mr. Miller," he continued, circling back like a hawk, "could it be possible you've mistaken my client for someone else? After all, red hair isn't uncommon."

"Possible, but not probable," Sam countered, his confidence unshaken. "I remember faces. It's part of my job, part of who I am. And I am certain about Ms. Chambers."

"Certainty is a luxury, Mr. Miller." The Defense attorney's words hung heavy, challenging the air itself.

"Truth isn't a luxury. It's a necessity," Sam shot back, his belief unyielding as steel.

"Indeed." The attorney backed away, the intensity of his scrutiny relenting for a moment.

"Nothing further," he concluded, his tactics exhausted against Sam's unwavering certainty.

Sam straightened, his gaze level. The Defense attorney loomed before him, a dark silhouette against the courtroom's stark light. Accusations hung in the air, sharp as knives.

"Mr. Miller," the attorney said, voice edged with insinuation, "could you be holding a grudge against Ms. Chambers? Is that why you're here today?"

"I'm here to tell the truth," Sam replied, unwavering. His hands steady, he met the attorney's eyes. "Nothing more."

The courtroom held its breath. The Defense attorney's shadow retreated, unsuccessful in shaking the foundation of Sam's resolve.

"Redirect, Your Honor," the Prosecution attorney announced, rising with purpose.

"Proceed," the judge nodded.

"Mr. Miller," the Prosecution began, her tone clear and direct, "tell us about the security measures at the costume shop. Did anything about the transaction with Ms. Chambers seem out of ordinary?"

"Every large transaction requires an ID check. It's policy," Sam stated matter-of-factly. He remembered Sheila's ID, her confident smirk as she handed it to him. "She was memorable. Red hair, green eyes. Couldn't mistake her."

"Did you follow this procedure with Ms. Chambers?"

"Without question." Confidence threaded through Sam's voice. "I checked her ID. She matched the photo. No doubt in my mind who I was dealing with."

"Thank you, Mr. Miller," the Prosecution said, nodding her approval.

"Nothing further, Your Honor."

"Very well." The judge surveyed the courtroom, impressed by the solidity of Sam's words.

Sam straightened, his fingers leaving the microphone as he addressed the courtroom. The Defense attorney loomed, a predator circling its prey. Yet Sam's voice didn't waver.

"Large cash transactions trigger an ID check. No exceptions," he said. His gaze didn't falter from the attorney's probing stare.

"Protocol was followed?" the attorney pressed, voice hinting at skepticism.

"Thoroughly." Sam's reply cut through the tension. "I checked her ID against her face. Sheila Chambers." He cast a brief glance towards Sheila, her green eyes a silent challenge.

"Her purchase, it was all above board, in line with store policy?" the Defense attorney prodded further, searching for cracks in the narrative.

"Entirely," Sam reaffirmed, his recollection clear as day. He recounted the procedure, the exchange of cash, the no-return policy she'd dismissed with a wave of her hand.

The Defense attorney paced, words measured, questions sharp. But Sam's story remained unscathed, his testimony a fortress.

"Nothing further," the attorney finally conceded. A rare flicker of doubt clouded his features as he returned to his seat.

The courtroom buzzed, sensing the shift. Sam's evidence stood firm, a beacon in the murky waters of the trial.

The Prosecution attorney rose, a swift motion that signaled the next act in this legal drama. Sam watched her approach, her heels clicking a steady rhythm against the courtroom's hushed silence.

"Mr. Miller," she began, voice crisp and clear, "for clarity, please restate the date of the transaction."

"June 5th," Sam replied, his tone matching the gravity of the question. Each word was measured, deliberate.

"Thank you." The attorney nodded, turning towards the jury with purpose. "And Ms. Chambers' demeanor during the purchase?"

"Excited," he recalled, "almost too eager to get her hands on the costume."

"Was there anything else about her behavior that struck you as unusual?"

Sam leaned into the microphone, his memory a spotlight. "She made a joke – said it was for a 'special occasion.'" His fingers gestured quotation marks, emphasizing the sarcasm that had tinged her words.

"Clear and consistent." The attorney's approval rang through the room. She swept a look over the jury, letting the significance of his testimony sink in.

"Nothing further, Your Honor," she concluded, confident in the weight of Sam's words.

"Thank you, Mr. Miller," the judge intoned, peering down at Sam over the rim of his glasses. His voice bore the timbre of seasoned authority. "Your testimony has been most illuminating."

Sam exhaled, a silent release. The judge's nod was all the acknowledgement he needed, the unspoken respect for the truth he'd provided.

"You are dismissed," the judge declared, his gavel a punctuation mark to Sam's role in the search for justice. The sound echoed, final and resolute.

Sam stepped back from the microphone, the buzz of the courtroom rising around him like a curtain call. His part was played; the stage now belonged to others.

Sam's shoes tapped against the polished courtroom floor, a steady rhythm marking his departure from the stand. He could feel the eyes of the jury on him, their gazes heavy with the weight of his words. Relief coursed through him, a palpable wave that washed away the tension knotted in his shoulders.

He glanced at Sheila Chambers, her piercing green eyes fixed on him, a silent challenge in their depths. But Sam's testimony was a fortress, its foundations laid in truth and detail. The red hair that had been so striking in the costume shop was now a beacon of guilt in the courtroom, undeniable and vivid.

His hands, once trembling, were now steady as he moved away from the microphone. His part was done. The facts were laid bare for the jury to dissect. As he reached his seat, the whispers of the courtroom buzzed around him—a hive of speculation and anticipation.

Sam settled into the hard, wooden chair, the sense of satisfaction anchoring him. He'd stood his ground, faced the defense's battering questions with the calm certainty of someone who knew he had nothing to hide. His memory had not faltered; the image of Sheila buying the clown outfit was etched into his mind, as clear as if it had happened moments ago.

The prosecutor's nod was subtle but filled with gratitude. They both knew the value of a credible witness. Sam watched as the attorney turned, ready to hammer the next nail into Sheila Chambers' coffin.

The judge's gavel brought the court back to order, but for Sam, the chaos of thoughts quieted. He'd played his role in the theater of the law, delivered his lines with conviction. Now it was up to the jury, those twelve arbiters of fate, to pen the final act.

As the courtroom drama unfolded, Sam's eyes drifted to the exit. Outside those doors, life would go on, the play would continue without him. But today, in this room, he'd given them a performance rooted in the stark reality of right and wrong. He'd been more than just a costume shop employee—he'd been a bearer of truth in the masquerade of justice.

Chapter 18

Mike's heartbeat hammered against his ribcage as he pushed through the steel doors into the prison visiting area. A cocktail of anticipation and anger coursed through his veins, each step echoing on the linoleum floor. Eyes darting from face to face, he searched for her.

There—Sheila, an island of calm in the sea of grey uniforms and anxious visitors. Clad in bold hues that clashed with the drab surroundings, she was impossible to miss. His jaw clenched tight, Mike felt a surge of adrenaline fuel his march across the room.

His polished shoes clicked with purpose, a steady drumbeat amidst the murmurs and shuffling feet. With every stride, Mike's fury built, a storm brewing beneath his composed exterior. He was a bullet train, unstoppable, fixated on his target.

As he closed in, Sheila's presence loomed larger, her confidence almost tangible. She sat there, queen of her tiny domain, unaware of the reckoning approaching. Mike's hands curled into fists, his fingernails digging crescents into his palms.

He reached the table, towering over her. The controlled fury in Mike's eyes reflected off the sterile tabletop. His presence demanded attention, a silent ultimatum hanging between them.

Sheila's gaze lifted, locking with Mike's. A smirk played on her lips, the corners of her mouth curling with smug satisfaction. Her eyes—a sharp green—shone, reflecting a cocktail of defiance and triumph. She leaned slightly forward, as if drawn by the gravity of his approach.

"Mike," she drawled, her voice oozing false warmth.

He said nothing, only narrowed his eyes. The space between them crackled with tension. Mike's hand shot out, slapping the table with a force that made the surface shudder. Heads turned, visitors' whispers hushed by the sudden display of aggression.

"Betrayal suits you, Sheila," he hissed through clenched teeth. His words were low but cut through the uneasy silence. Every syllable dripped with accusation, his anger barely leashed.

Sheila's smile didn't falter, a testament to her brazen nerve. Mike's heart pounded, each beat a drum sounding the charge for justice.

Sheila reclined, the metal chair creaking under her weight. Her expression was a fortress, impervious to Mike's onslaught. "Mike," she began, voice steady as steel, "if only you had tread more carefully." She tilted her head, regarding him like a chess player would a novice opponent. "You left tracks too wide for any cover-up."

Mike felt his jaw tighten, the muscles taut as bowstrings. The accusation hung in the air, a noxious cloud. He leaned closer, his voice climbing an octave, sharp as shattered glass. "Careless?" he spat out, the word bitter on his tongue. "Your plans were Swiss cheese, Sheila. Full of holes."

The surrounding whispers faded into nothingness. Eyes darted back and forth between them, spectators to a gladiatorial bout. Mike's chest heaved with each breath, his heart a relentless hammer against his ribcage. Sheila's composure was a slap across his face—calm, collected, as if discussing the weather rather than their crumbling empire of deceit.

"Reckless," he accused, the word a bullet fired at point-blank range. His indignation was a living thing, clawing its way out of his throat. "That's what you were. A bull in the china shop of our plans."

Sheila's lips twitched, the ghost of a smirk. Her confidence was a blade, and Mike felt it edge closer to his resolve, threatening to draw blood.

Sheila's gaze sharpened, her eyes slicing through Mike's defenses. "Oh, Mikey," she cooed, the words laced with venom. "You never did grasp the grand scheme of things." A chuckle, cold and hollow, escaped her lips. She leaned in, her voice a whisper wrapped in thorns. "I planned Marlene's end to the last breath. You were merely a puppet."

Her taunt was a gut punch, cruel and precise. Mike's hands balled into fists, his knuckles whitening. The room seemed to shrink around him, the walls closing in. Sheila had played him—a maestro conducting a symphony of betrayal.

"Impossible," he muttered, but his voice cracked. Doubt crept in, a relentless tide. Anger flared within him, hot and blinding, but fear followed close behind. Each word from Sheila unraveled his reality, thread by thread.

He stood there, a man carved from frustration and dismay. His face twisted, the lines deepening with each passing second. He saw it now—the careful steps she took, the traps laid bare. Mike had walked right into them, blind and trusting.

"Marlene trusted you," he said, the words scraping his throat raw. But they were a whisper against the storm Sheila had conjured. She had orchestrated the unspeakable, and he had been her unwitting accomplice. His heart pounded—a drumbeat of guilt.

Sheila's posture shifted, a predator closing in on its prey. She leaned forward across the cold metal table, her voice slicing through the air, low and menacing. "You see, Mike, I won," she hissed, her green eyes alight with malice. "I pulled the strings, and you danced."

Mike's chest tightened, breaths shallow and sharp. The words hit him like a physical blow. Marlene's gentle smile flashed before his eyes, haunting him. "How can you sit there, so smug, knowing what you've done?" His voice trembled, anger and sorrow battling for dominance.

"You took a life, Sheila. Marlene's life." He choked on the next words, each one heavier than the last. "Her family... those kids. They're broken because of us." Regret seeped into his tone, thick and suffocating.

Sheila's smirk remained, untouched by the gravity of his words. Her victory was all that mattered in her twisted game. Mike's hands shook at his sides, fists of fury restrained by sheer will. The weight of his guilt bore down on him, a relentless force crushing his resolve.

"Look at you," he spat, "reveling in the wreckage. Is this what you wanted?"

Her only response was the glint of triumph in her eyes, a silent testament to the chaos she had wrought. Every word from her was a nail in the coffin of his conscience. Marlene deserved better. They all did. And Mike was left to grapple with the ruins of a life he helped shatter.

Her laughter split the silence, a cold, jarring cackle that bounced off the sterile walls of the prison visiting area. Sheila's amusement was a blade twisting in Mike's gut, the sound clawing at his insides. She was mocking him, mocking the pain, the loss, the destruction they had caused.

"Pathetic," she sneered, her voice slicing through the hum of whispered conversations and clinking vending machines. "You think your guilt means anything now?"

Mike felt the shiver run down his spine, the echo of her laughter haunting him. This was the woman he had trusted, the woman he had schemed with. And here she sat, delighting in the turmoil they had unleashed upon an unsuspecting family. Her joy was grotesque, a twisted reflection of the soul he suspected she never possessed.

The visitors around them cast furtive glances, sensing the tension rising like a storm. But none of it touched Sheila. She was in her element, thriving on the chaos she had sown with such precision.

Mike's fists balled at his sides. His jaw clenched so tight it hurt. The fury within him burned hot and fierce, a wildfire threatening to consume him. It was too much—her callousness, her pride in their shared sin—it was all too much.

"Enough." The word was a growl, torn from the depths of his being. He couldn't sit there, not for another second, not with her.

He stood abruptly, the legs of the chair screeching against the floor as if in protest. The sound was loud, disruptive, drawing more eyes to their isolated corner of the room. But Mike didn't care. His gaze locked onto Sheila's, a silent battle of wills. Anger smoldered in his eyes, mixed with a resignation that felt like defeat.

Sheila's expression remained unchanged, her smug smile a mask that revealed nothing of the darkness behind it. Mike turned away from her, from the monster she had shown herself to be. Every step he took felt heavy, burdened by the weight of what he knew, what he had done, and the impossibility of ever making it right.

Mike's back was to her now, every line of his broad shoulders radiating finality. Sheila's gaze followed him, her smile never wavering, a serpent basking in the aftermath of its venomous bite. She knew the wound was deep; she had made sure of it.

Her lips curled upwards, satisfaction oozing from every pore. The eyes that watched Mike's retreat gleamed with malice. In her twisted game, this was a checkmate.

Mike felt the eyes on him—burning holes—but he didn't look back. Each step was a declaration, a severing of ties. The weight of what he'd become anchored his feet, made each movement an effort against the mire of his own making.

The air around him thickened with the stench of guilt, a noxious cloud that clung to his skin. Justice had come at a price and the currency was his conscience. He'd paid in full now, the transaction etched into his soul.

Mike left behind the click of Sheila's mocking laughter, the cold walls of the prison echoing the sound long after he'd gone. Her twisted smile haunted the edges of his mind, a specter that would not easily be exorcised.

The heavy door clanged shut behind Mike. Freedom, tainted. The chill of the corridor seeped into his bones as he walked, his pace brisk, a man propelled by an unseen force. A cacophony of locks and buzzers punctuated his exit, each sound a reminder of the prison he carried within himself.

Outside, daylight assaulted his senses. He squinted, eyes adjusting to the unfiltered glare of the sun. People passed by, their lives untainted by the shadow that loomed over him. How easy it was for them, unknowing, untouched by the vile undercurrents that dictated his existence.

Mike's jaw clenched. The bitter taste of regret lingered on his tongue, thick and choking. Memories flashed—Marlene's lifeless eyes, Sheila's venomous smirk—their images swirling in a dance of accusation.

He paused, took a deep breath. Air, heavy with exhaust fumes and city grime, filled his lungs. It was the same world, yet nothing was the same. Not anymore. Every step forward etched a line of separation from the man he once was.

The path ahead loomed long, uncertain. Redemption was a mere speck on the horizon, a destination shrouded in doubt. Could a man like him tread such a path? Was there a penance sufficient for the pain he'd caused?

Mike's hand brushed the fabric of his tailored suit, a costume now, an ill-fitting remnant of a life built on deception. The sharp contours of his polished shoes mocked him with every step. They were the shoes of a successful businessman; they were the shoes of a fraud.

His face, once the visage of confidence, now bore the cracks of his fractured soul. Anger wrestled with sorrow, each emotion carving its mark for the world to see. To passersby, he might have been just another man battling the woes of life. But Mike knew the depth of his turmoil ran far deeper.

He moved through the city's pulse, its rhythm alien to his own. Cars honked, people shouted, life went on around him—a stark contrast to the stagnation in his heart.

As the distance from the prison lengthened, so did the shadow of Sheila's influence. Yet her laughter, that chilling echo, refused to be left behind. It was a specter, haunting his steps, a ghost he would carry to the end of his days.

Mike's resolve hardened. His sins were many, but his determination was newfound. If there was a way to make amends, to carve a sliver of good from the wreckage he'd wrought, he would find it.

For now, he walked. Away from the prison, away from Sheila, towards a future unwritten. Each step was a commitment, a silent vow echoing off the concrete jungle around him. The road to redemption began here, beneath the weight of guilt, under the scrutiny of a world indifferent to his plight.

Chapter 19

Daniel sat rigid on the worn sofa, the fabric threads bearing witness to decades of family life now hushed in mourning. He was alone in the house he once filled with laughter, every corner a stark reminder of what was lost. His mother's cheerful knick-knacks gathered dust, mocking the stillness. Clenching his fists, Daniel's knuckles whitened, mirroring the resolve hardening in his dark eyes.

He flipped open his laptop, its glow casting eerie shadows across the room. Click after click, his search history a testament to sleepless nights and relentless pursuit. Today's headlines held a new promise; they had to. His pulse quickened as the page loaded, anticipation threading through him like electricity.

"Local Woman Arrested, Pleads Guilty." The words blazed across the screen, seizing his breath. Sheila's name followed, bold and unyielding. Daniel scanned the article, each sentence another weight lifted, another step toward vindication. The image of Sheila, her striking red hair now caged behind bars, seemed to sneer at him from the pixels.

"Got you," he muttered under his breath, his heart racing with a turbulent mix of triumph and raw, unprocessed grief.

Daniel's jaw clenched tight as the words of the sentencing blurred before his eyes. Life without parole. The screen seemed to pulse with a vindictive heartbeat, echoing his own. Satisfaction seared through the cold coil of anger in his gut, yet the hollow space where grief lay whispered that no sentence could return what had been stolen from him.

He read on, each detail a jagged piece of the night his mother was taken. His fists trembled, not just with the fury of a son robbed of love but with the bitter relief of knowing her killer would face justice. The digital paragraphs detailed Sheila's downfall—a symphony of legalese that sang both vengeance and sorrow into the quiet room.

In the break room of the precinct, Brian and Jessica sat across from each other, their coffee cups steaming faintly between them. They exchanged a glance over the rim of their mugs—a silent conversation passing in their weary eyes. It was done. The case that had consumed their days and haunted their nights had found its grim resolution.

The murmur of the station buzzed around them, but in this pocket of stillness, they allowed themselves that brief nod, an acknowledgment of closure not just for themselves but for a son who had become the embodiment of loss and persistence. They sipped their coffee, the bitter warmth a small comfort against the backdrop of the justice system's stark reality.

Brian leaned back, the chair protesting with a familiar creak. His arms crossed over his chest, eyes fixed on a spot on the ceiling. Countless hours spent sifting through evidence sprawled across his mind's eye like a vast puzzle finally pieced together. The relief was tangible, settling into his muscles with a weight that felt oddly comforting. Marlene's gentle smile haunted him, but there was solace in knowing her killer wouldn't walk free.

"Can you believe it?" Jessica broke through his reverie, leaning forward. Her eyes sparkled, alight with an earnest fire. "We did it, Brian."

Her voice carried a mix of pride and gratitude, and she paused, collecting her thoughts. "This case... it changed me. Taught me so much." She offered a smile, one that seemed to acknowledge the gravity of their achievement.

"Thank you," she continued, sincerity etching every word. "For letting me be a part of this, for guiding me. It's made all the difference."

Brian nodded, recognizing the milestone this case represented in her young career. Her growth from eager rookie to tenacious officer hadn't gone unnoticed. She was becoming the kind of cop he knew the force needed—dedicated, perceptive, relentless.

"Good work, Lee," he said simply, his tone firm yet layered with unspoken respect. "You've earned your stripes on this one."

Brian swirled the last of his coffee in the bottom of the mug, the dark liquid mirroring the late nights and early mornings that had been a constant companion. "It's more than just solving a case, Lee," he said, his voice carrying the weight of experience." It's about restoring balance. Every time we put away someone like Sheila, we're tipping the scales back towards justice."

Jessica nodded, her brown eyes reflecting the fluorescent lights above. "Every victim matters," she affirmed, her tone steady and resolute. "Marlene's case, it sends a message. To the community. To the predators out there. We don't rest until justice is served."

"Exactly." Brian set down his mug with finality. "It's not just closure for the family; it's a win for the neighborhood, for the city. We're the thin blue line, Lee. Remember that."

They sat in silence for a moment, the gravity of their words hanging between them. Then, releasing a slow breath, Jessica rose from the table, her posture speaking to the determination that defined her.

Scene transitioned.

Across the town, in the stillness of his childhood home, Daniel pushed himself up from the chair. His limbs felt heavy, burdened by grief yet propelled by an inner force that refused to yield. He moved across the room, steps silent against the worn carpet.

The shelf loomed before him, a repository of frozen moments. Carefully, he reached out, his fingers brushing over the edges of the frames. Images of his mother smiled back at him, each one a testament to a life stolen too soon. "I won't let this be in vain," he whispered to her smiling visage. "Your story isn't over, not while I'm here to tell it."

With every photograph he touched, his resolve hardened, each promise a vow etched into the core of who he was. Daniel Thompson, son of Marlene, would carry her legacy forward. He would ensure the world knew her name, knew her life mattered.

Daniel knelt beside the box, its cardboard flaps open like a gaping mouth ready to swallow the remnants of his mother's life. He picked up her sweaters, still faintly carrying her scent, and folded them with precision before placing them gently inside. Each item was a memory, a thread in the tapestry of their shared existence.

A photograph slipped from between the pages of an old novel. Daniel caught it before it could drift to the floor. His thumb grazed the glossy surface, over the faces frozen in time. It was a snapshot of happier days, his parents arm in arm, eyes bright with laughter. The image stung, a sharp jab to his heart. He tucked it safely into the box, atop the layers of clothing and bits of ephemera that made up Marlene's earthly possessions.

His hands were steady, but his heart thrummed with an undercurrent of sorrow. This ritual of packing was cathartic, a physical manifestation of organizing the chaos that grief had wrought. Each object placed in the box was an acknowledgement of loss, but also a step towards healing.

With the last of her belongings nestled inside, Daniel pressed the flaps of the box together. The roll of tape screeched as he pulled it free, sealing the cardboard with a firm swipe. The sound echoed in the quiet room, a full stop at the end of a long, harrowing sentence.

He sat back on his heels, surveying the stack of boxes that now contained his mother's world. His breath hitched, a momentary hitch in the otherwise steady rhythm of his resolve. Daniel lifted the family portrait from the mantle. Their smiles seemed to reach out to him, a silent chorus of encouragement.

"Goodbye, Mom," he murmured, tracing the outline of her face with a fingertip.

The click of the frame as it settled among the rest of her things was a soft but definitive note of closure. Daniel stood, shoulders squared, facing the reality of a world without her. The sealed boxes were more than just containers; they were guardians of the past, custodians of the love and life that would move forward with him, even as this chapter came to an end.

Brian pushed back his chair, the legs scraping against the linoleum with a sound that signaled the end of a brief respite. He stood up, straightening his tie with quick, efficient motions. Jessica mirrored him, her posture straight as she rose, her eyes locking onto his with an intensity that spoke volumes.

They exchanged a silent nod, the weight of their shared experiences pressing down on them like a tangible force. It was a mutual recognition—their relentless pursuit had not been in vain. Marlene's case was closed, justice served. Still, the unspoken understanding hung in the air: there were more battles ahead, more wrongs to right.

With that unspoken promise lingering between them, Brian turned towards the door. His steps were measured, the rhythm of a man who knew this dance all too well. Jessica fell into step beside him, her stride confident, her youth doing nothing to diminish the authority she carried.

They passed through the break room doorway, leaving behind the scent of stale coffee and the ghostly echoes of hushed conversations. The hallway stretched out before them, lined with doors that held stories yet to be told, secrets begging to be unearthed.

As they walked, Brian's keen intellect shifted gears, already sifting through the details of the next case file that awaited him. Jessica's thoughts raced alongside his, her observational skills honing in on every detail, every nuance. Together, they moved through the precinct—a seamless unit bound by duty and an unwavering commitment to the badge.

Their steps echoed off the walls, the sound a steady drumbeat against the undercurrent of activity that thrived within these walls. Detectives huddled in corners, uniforms brushed past with purpose, and the faint chatter of dispatchers filled the air.

The break room door swung shut behind them, its click a punctuation mark to the silent vow they'd taken. Onward they went, Brian Hayes and Jessica Lee, ready to tackle whatever lay ahead. Their journey for justice was far from over; it beckoned them forward with the promise of new cases, new challenges. And they answered the call, as they always did, with purposeful determination etched into every step.

The precinct doors closed behind them with an air of finality. Brian paused, taking in the weight of Marlene Thompson's case—a weight lifted, yet its imprint enduring. He reflected on the justice served, a chapter concluded in the relentless narrative of crime and retribution.

"Good work," he said, his voice low and gruff, punctuated by the gravity of their accomplishment.

"Thanks to you, too," Jessica replied, her tone acknowledging their shared victory. Her gaze lingered on the doors that had just swung shut, the barrier between the chaos they quelled and the order they sought to maintain.

Daniel's face flashed through Brian's mind—haunted yet hopeful. The young man had found solace in the outcome, a semblance of peace in the unyielding storm of loss. The detective knew the power of closure, how it could mend fences in fractured lives.

"Marlene's case... it changed things," Jessica remarked, her voice tinged with a mixture of reverence and resolve.

"It did," Brian agreed, his nod affirming her sentiment. "But there will be others. There always are."

They stood side by side, the hum of the precinct enveloping them—a symphony of phones ringing, keyboards clacking, radios crackling. It was the soundtrack of justice, unending and uncompromising.

"Ready for what's next?" Brian asked, his eyes scanning the horizon of their shared path.

"Always," Jessica answered without hesitation. Her stance confident, her determination palpable.

They stepped forward, the rhythm of their movement synchronized with the pulse of duty. Cases would come and go, but their purpose remained steadfast—to chase the truth, to stand in defense of those who had fallen.

Don't miss out!

Visit the website below and you can sign up to receive emails whenever Shane Reed publishes a new book. There's no charge and no obligation.

https://books2read.com/r/B-A-LSDAB-VHIIF

BOOKS 2 READ

Connecting independent readers to independent writers.

Did you love *Clown Killer*? Then you should read *Voices Of Deception*[1] by Shane Reed!

[2]

In a world where the line between sanity and madness blurs, Vince was just an ordinary Canadian man—until the day a sinister voice claimed to be his god. Tasked with a divine mission to protect humanity from an impending alien threat, Vince spirals into a nightmarish quest where reality twists and darkness reigns.

As the voice drives him deeper into paranoia, Vince becomes convinced that extraterrestrial beings are disguised as ordinary people. His frantic search leads him to abandon his life, leaving behind a shattered marriage and a desperate wife who can no longer comprehend the man he has become.

---

1. https://books2read.com/u/47BKW8

2. https://books2read.com/u/47BKW8

On a fateful bus ride, Vince's delusions reach a horrifying climax when he identifies a fellow passenger, Tim, as the very alien he was meant to destroy. What follows is a brutal act of violence that will haunt him forever—a gruesome murder fueled by an unrelenting command from a god of his own making.

In the aftermath, Vince faces the consequences of a mind unraveling under the weight of untreated mental illness. Committed to a psychiatric facility, he spends seven agonizing years grappling with the echoes of his actions. Now, as he steps back into a world that once seemed so familiar, Vince must confront the chilling truth of his past and the haunting specter of the life he extinguished.

"Voices Of Deception" *is a harrowing tale of the fragile human mind, exploring the depths of delusion, the horror of unchecked mental illness, and the chilling intersection between faith and fanaticism. Will Vince ever find redemption, or is he forever bound by the shadows of his own creation?*

Also by Shane Reed

A Conning Couple Novel
Checkmate
The Great Escape
The Queen's Gambit
The Sicilian Defense
Fool's Mate
The Scottish Game
Stale Mate
The Conning Couple Books 1-5

True Crime
The Sniffing Dog Scam
The Vengeful Parent
The Psychic Scam
Conterfeit Capitalist
Innocence On Trial
The Deceptive Dream
Voices Of Deception
Shadows of a Perfect Life
Unjust Conviction
Clown Killer